Carver's Head Was Spinning.

Standing at his front door was a beautiful woman who *said* she was a social worker. And clutching her by the hand was a twelve-year-old girl who looked jarringly familiar.

"Who are you?" he asked.

"Maddy Garrett," she replied matter of factly. "This is Rachel Stillman."

"Rachel...Stillman?"

"Daughter of Abigail Stillman," she said, as if that would explain everything.

"I don't know anyone named Abigail Stillman."

The bright smile Maddy had been wearing fell. "Hasn't anyone contacted you about this?" she asked.

"About what?" Carver mumbled.

"About the child Abigail Stillman has—er—left behind. According to the birth certificate, you're the girl's father."

"Ex-excuse me?" he stammered. "I'm what?"

"Congratulations, Mr. Venner," Maddy said dryly. "It's a girl."

FROM HERE TO PATERNITY: These three men weren't expecting to become parents—and fatherhood isn't the only thing the stork delivered!

Dear Reader,

Can you believe that for the next three months we'll be celebrating the publication of the 1000th Silhouette Desire? That's quite a milestone! The festivities begin this month with six books by some of your longtime favorites and exciting new names in romance.

We'll continue into next month, May, with the actual publication of Book #1000—by Diana Palmer—and then we'll keep the fun going into June. There's just so much going on that I can't put it all into one letter. You'll just have to keep reading!

This month we have an absolutely terrific lineup, beginning with *Saddle Up*, a MAN OF THE MONTH by Mary Lynn Baxter. There's also *The Groom, I Presume?*— the latest in Annette Broadrick's DAUGHTERS OF TEXAS miniseries. *Father of the Brat* launches the new FROM HERE TO PATERNITY miniseries by Elizabeth Bevarly, and *Forgotten Vows* by Modean Moon is the first of three books about what happens on THE WEDDING NIGHT. Lass Small brings us her very own delightful sense of humor in *A Stranger in Texas*. And our DEBUT AUTHOR this month is Anne Eames with *Two Weddings and a Bride*.

And next month, as promised, Book #1000, a MAN OF THE MONTH, *Man of Ice* by Diana Palmer!

Lucia Macro,
Senior Editor

Please address questions and book requests to:
Silhouette Reader Service
U.S.: 3010 Walden Ave., P.O. Box 1325, Buffalo, NY 14269
Canadian: P.O. Box 609, Fort Erie, Ont. L2A 5X3

ELIZABETH BEVARLY
FATHER OF THE BRAT

SILHOUETTE *Desire*®

Published by Silhouette Books

America's Publisher of Contemporary Romance

With much love, for Dorothy and Harold Stucker
(aka Aunt Dot and Uncle Washie).
You're the best second set of parents a kid could have.

 SILHOUETTE BOOKS

ISBN 0-373-05993-0

FATHER OF THE BRAT

Copyright © 1996 by Elizabeth Bevarly

ELIZABETH BEVARLY

is an honors graduate of the University of Louisville and achieved her dream of writing full-time before she even turned thirty! At heart, she is also an avid voyager who once helped navigate a friend's thirty-five-foot sailboat across the Bermuda Triangle. "I really love to travel," says this self-avowed beach bum. "To me, it's the best education a person can give to herself." Her dream is to one day have her own sailboat, a beautifully renovated older-model forty-two-footer, and to enjoy the freedom and tranquillity seafaring can bring. Elizabeth likes to think she has a lot in common with the characters she creates, people who know love and life go hand in hand. And she's getting some firsthand experience with maternity as well—she and her husband recently welcomed their firstborn baby, a son.

Dear Reader,

When I first discovered I was going to be included in **Celebration 1000**, I experienced an immediate flashback to college, when I was living in my parents' basement, reading my very first Silhouette Desire. I had received it after responding to a Silhouette ad in *Cosmopolitan* magazine (I was very cosmopolitan in college, you see), and after reading the last page of the novel, I thought, "Wow, where have these books been all my life?"

I was in my final year of earning a B.A. in English, Yet nothing I had studied came close to leaving me with the sense of contentment that I received from that single red book.

I started reading every Desire I could get my hands on. And eventually, because I had always wanted to be a novelist, romance was what came out when I sat down to write my first book. It amazes me still to realize that I'm now responsible for creating the kind of books that provided me with so much for so long—romance, adventure, escape…and those wonderful happy endings that even a degree in English couldn't stop making me crave.

I'm so delighted to be included in **Celebration 1000**. I'm not sure I can adequately describe what it means to be keeping literary company with the novelists I've always admired, to be and writing for a publisher and a line of books I've always loved—to be a part of the festivities surrounding the publication of the 1000th Desire… Somehow, it fills me with a sense of completion and satisfaction that I haven't found anywhere else.

For years, Silhouette Desire has brought me unrivaled reading pleasure. Now the folks at Silhouette provide me with unrivaled writing pleasure, too. And I can only hope you enjoy reading my books as much as I enjoy writing them.

Very best wishes,

Elizabeth Bevarly

One

Carver Venner was beat. In the last seventy-two hours, he'd logged over eight thousand miles on his frequent flyer account, had been slapped in the face, kicked in the shins, bitten by an angry cat and shocked by an electric fence. He'd been shot at—twice—and called a filthy, stinking capitalist, an imperialist dog and a lousy tipper. He'd survived a taxi ride in a town that had few—if any—traffic laws, had eaten food he'd been hard-pressed to identify—which in itself was probably a blessing—and had somehow stumbled onto a literal den of thieves. He had a stubbed toe and a throbbing hangnail, and he could scarcely remember the last time he'd slept.

Man, the life of a journalist hadn't turned out to be anything at all like he'd thought it would be when he'd enrolled at Columbia University twenty years ago.

How he'd managed to make it back to his South Philadelphia apartment in one piece was some vague memory he knew he was going to have to write up tomorrow. For now, though, he dropped his battered, ragged duffel bag in the middle of his bedroom floor and fell backward onto his bed with a sigh. Almost as an afterthought, he sat up to skim off his faded green polo, then found himself too exhausted to bother with the blue jeans and hiking boots he'd also been wearing since yesterday morning. Instead, he dropped onto his back again.

Sleep, he thought. Finally, finally, he could get some real sleep. He ran a restless hand over the three-day stubble of beard on his face, shoved his overly long, dark brown hair from his forehead and closed his eyes. He was just about to lose himself in the welcome relief of slumber when some-one—someone who obviously had a death wish—launched into a ceaseless pounding on his front door.

"Dammit," he muttered without moving. Maybe who-ever the someone was would go away, and then he wouldn't have to kill them after all.

But whoever it was keeping him from sleep did indeed seem to have suicidal tendencies, because the knocking just increased more loudly.

Carver sighed again, jackknifed up from his bed and staggered out to his living room. He flattened one big hand against the front door and curled the other over the knob, then stood with his chin dropped to his chest and one final hope that his visitor had gone away. But the rapping started again, even more annoying than it had been before, so he jerked the door open hard.

"What?" he barked. "What is it?"

A woman stood in the hall with her curled fingers poised at shoulder level. She was about to knock again, something that would have landed her fist in the middle of Carver's naked chest, but she stopped herself just shy of completing the action and dropped her hand quickly back to her side. In the other hand, she carried a battered leather satchel not unlike the kind elementary schoolchildren had carried way back when Carver was young enough to have been one of them himself.

She was a good foot shorter than he, her black hair lib-erally threaded with silver and cropped shorter than his own.

She wore round, tortoiseshell-rimmed glasses that made her brown eyes appear huge, and a shapeless olive drab trench coat over a white, baggy, man-styled shirt and brown, even baggier, man-styled trousers. Her only concession to her femininity was a filigreed antique brooch pinned at her collar and matching earrings that dangled from her ears.

She was in no way the kind of woman with whom Carver normally associated. But somehow she looked very familiar.

"Carver Venner?" she asked in a no-nonsense voice of efficiency that immediately grated on his nerves.

"Yeah, that's me."

"I'm with the Child Welfare Office. I've been assigned to your case."

Okay, he was tired, Carver thought as he studied the woman harder, still trying to place where he might have met her. But there was no way he was so tired that he had forgotten about the presence of a child in his life.

"I beg your pardon?" he asked.

"Your daughter," she clarified, aiding him not at all. "I'm here to assist the two of you—to help you get acquainted and settled in."

He closed his eyes and shook his head, trying to wake himself from what was one of the most bizarre dreams he'd ever had. Unfortunately, when he opened his eyes again, he was still standing in front of his open door, and the oddly familiar woman was still staring at him.

"Do I know you?" he asked.

Her eyes widened for a moment in what he could only liken to panic, something that just compounded his confusion. Without replying, she lifted her satchel and flipped it open, shoved her hand inside and withdrew a pristine, white business card.

M. H. Garrett, L.C.S.W., it read in bold black type. *Caseworker, Child Welfare Office of Pennsylvania.* It was decorated with the official state seal and seemed to be legitimate.

M. H. Garrett, he repeated to himself. Nope, not a name that rang any bells. "What's the M.H. stand for?"

"Mostly Harmless," she told him without missing a beat.

He glanced up at the woman again only to find her staring back at him in silence, daring him to press the issue. Dammit, even her prissy voice was familiar. He was sure he knew her from somewhere, he just couldn't remember where. It was about to drive him crazier than he already felt when he recalled that she had just accused him of having a daughter.

He smiled wryly. "I think somebody got their wires crossed somewhere, Ms. Garrett. I don't have a daughter. In fact, I've never even been married, so it doesn't seem likely that there's a little Venner kid out there running around somewhere."

M. H. Garrett, Caseworker, narrowed her eyes at Carver and stuck her hand back into her satchel, this time pulling out a very thick, very well used binder. She flipped through it easily until she found whatever she had been looking for, scanned a few pages, then looked up at Carver again.

"Rachel Stillman," she said, as if those two words would explain everything.

Carver shook his head. "Sorry, never heard of her."

Mostly Harmless Garrett eyed him warily. "She's your daughter, Mr. Venner."

"No, she isn't."

"Yes, she is."

He chuckled, feeling more and more bizarre with every passing moment. "Oh, come on. She doesn't even have the same last name as me. Boy, you folks at Welfare really are overworked." He relented when he saw her lips thin into a tight line. "I assure you, Ms. Garrett, that I do not have a daughter named Rachel anything. Somebody at your office has sent you on a wild-goose chase."

The caseworker glanced down at her notebook again. "Abigail Stillman," she said this time.

Carver was about to tell her that he didn't have a daughter named Abigail Stillman, either, when he remembered that he did in fact know someone by that name. Or rather, he used to know someone by that name. Another journalist he'd met in Guatemala about ten or twelve years ago. The two of them had shared a very hot, very heavy, very brief affair. One week, he recalled now, unable to halt the lascivious smile that curled his lips. And what a week it had been.

"Okay, I do know an Abby Stillman," he told M. H. Garrett, still smiling at his heated memories. "But I haven't heard from her in years. Have you seen her recently? How is she?"

"She's dead."

His smile fell, and something raw and hot knotted in his stomach. "She's what?"

"She's dead, Mr. Venner. A car accident. Drunk driver. She was killed instantly." The caseworker shifted from one foot to the other a little uncomfortably. "Uh, hasn't anyone contacted you about this?"

Still feeling as if someone had just kicked him in the groin, Carver mumbled, "About what?"

M. H. Garrett pressed her free hand against her forehead and rubbed hard. "About Abigail Stillman. About the child she left behind—a twelve-year-old girl named Rachel." She dropped her hand back to her side and studied him for a moment before continuing. "According to the girl's birth certificate...um...you're her father."

Carver's eyebrows shot up at that. "Ex...excuse me?" he stammered. "I'm what?"

M. H. Garrett bit her lip and tried—without much success—to smile. "Congratulations, Mr. Venner," she said, clearly striving for a levity she didn't feel. "It's a girl."

"Whoa, whoa, whoa, whoa, whoa," Carver objected, holding up his hand as if he could stop her announcement. "That's impossible. I couldn't...I mean, Abby didn't...and I sure as hell..." His voice trailed off and he stared at the woman in the hall. "This can't be happening," he finally concluded.

"Maybe I better come in and try to sort things out," the social worker offered. "Someone was supposed to have contacted you by now, but obviously no one has. I'm sure you have some questions, and maybe—"

"Questions?" he sputtered. "Questions? You're damned right I have some questions. Not to mention a few choice words."

The woman stiffened immediately and pointed a finger at him. Somehow, even before she started wagging it at him, Carver was certain that that was precisely what she was going to do.

"Look, don't take this out on me," she said with a vigorous shake of her finger. "I'm just trying to do my job."

He nodded slowly and tried to calm himself. "You're right. I'm sorry. It's just that this is a little...uh... surprising, to say the least. There's obviously been some mistake. There's no way I could be this girl's father."

M. H. Garrett eyed him thoughtfully for a moment before asking, "So you and Abigail Stillman never...?"

"Never what?"

The caseworker looked uncomfortable again. "Never... um, you know."

"Know what?"

"Never had...relations?"

"Relations?"

The woman sighed fitfully, and he could swear she was blushing. "Of a, um, of a sexual nature?"

Finally Carver understood. "Oh, sure, we...uh...we had relations. Quite a few times if memory serves, but—"

"I see." M. H. Garrett frowned her disapproval.

Carver didn't like her tone of voice one bit. "No, you don't see," he insisted. "I'm not this kid's father."

The caseworker sighed heavily and tilted her head forward, toward the inside of his apartment. "Maybe I should come in and try to get all this straightened out. I can't imagine why no one at Welfare has contacted you before now, especially with the child arriving tomorrow, but maybe—"

"Tomorrow?" he repeated. "This kid's coming to Philadelphia tomorrow? But I'm not her father."

"—but maybe we can get it all straightened out without too much trouble," the woman finished as if Carver had never spoken.

He wanted to slam the door in her face, wanted to go back to bed for some much needed sleep and forget that this surreal encounter had ever occurred. Unfortunately, M. H. Garrett's expression assured him she wasn't going anywhere until this thing was settled. Reluctantly, he moved aside for her to enter. As she passed him, he caught a whiff of her perfume, a rich, floral fragrance that seemed an unlikely choice for her. He liked it, though, and was pretty sure it was gardenia. His sister, Sylvie, wore a similar scent.

Impulsively, he reached for his shirt pocket, where he kept his cigarettes, and when his fingers encountered only flesh and hair, he suddenly remembered that he was only half dressed. Feeling inexplicably embarrassed by the realization, Carver began a hasty retreat to his bedroom.

"Uh, let me just go put on a shirt," he said, thrusting a thumb over his shoulder in the direction he was already headed. "I'll only be a minute."

When M. H. Garrett seemed to be relieved by his decision, he got the strangest impression that it wasn't so much because she was offended by his lack of clothing as it was because she was fascinated by it.

Lack of sleep, he remembered, could give a person the craziest sensations.

He returned to the living room inhaling deeply on a much needed cigarette and buttoning up a well-worn, plaid flannel shirt that he didn't bother to tuck in. The woman from the Child Welfare Office had discarded her trench coat on the coatrack by the door and sat in the middle of his couch with a number of official-looking documents spread out on his coffee table. Carver's furnishings were sparse at best—second and third-hand castoffs he'd picked up at garage sales and flea markets. His things were inexpensive, functional and no-frills. And somehow, the woman sitting among them fit right in.

"Can I get you anything?" he asked her as he headed into the adjoining kitchen. Although he felt as if a good, stiff shot of whiskey was probably more appropriate for the bomb she had just dropped, coffee was what he was craving most. "Coffee? Tea? Soda?"

"Whatever you're having will be fine," she said.

"I'll just be a minute."

While the coffeemaker wheezed and dripped laconically, Carver returned to the living room to find the infuriatingly familiar Ms. Garrett reading over a file. He wished he could remember where he knew her from, couldn't quell the certainty that the two of them shared some kind of significant history. But her name was in no way recognizable, and she wasn't at all the kind of woman he normally dated. He'd never had any cause to work with the Child Welfare Office, and couldn't imagine anyplace else he might have met her. Maybe she was a friend of one of his sisters, he thought. Though even that seemed unlikely. She just appeared to be too straitlaced to be someone who would run around with Livy or Sylvie.

He stubbed out his cigarette in an ashtray after using it to light a second. "I'm sorry," he said as he expelled an errant stream of smoke from his lungs, "but I just can't shake the feeling that I know you from somewhere."

The woman glanced up quickly at his statement, and he could almost swear she looked panicky again. Her reaction made no sense, but he couldn't dissuade himself of the feeling that he'd put her on edge somehow. Then she frowned, waving her hand in front of her face to dispel the cigarette smoke he had inadvertently sent her way, and he understood her agitation. Mumbling an apology, he stubbed out the second cigarette, as well.

"And where might we have met, Mr. Venner?" she asked as she watched him perform the action. He could almost feel her disapproval of what was only one of his many bad habits, and he wondered why he cared.

"See, now that's the sixty-four thousand dollar question," he told her as he took his seat in a chair opposite the couch. "Can you help me out?"

She smiled briefly and looked back down at her pile of information. "No, sorry, I can't."

"Can't or won't?" Somehow, he suspected the latter was true.

Her head snapped up again, and she glared at him. That glare, more than anything else she had done since he'd opened his front door, made Carver even more certain that he did in fact know her. Unfortunately, a lot of women had glared at him in his time. For some reason, this woman just seemed to be better at it than most.

"I have a copy of Rachel Stillman's birth certificate along with some other documents," she said, ignoring his question. "From the state of California. They clearly indicate that you are the girl's father."

Carver frowned. "Let me see those." He took the collection of papers she extended toward him. They, too, appeared to be legitimate documents, complete with raised seals and indecipherable signatures. The birth certificate stated quite clearly in black and white that a female child named Rachel Carver Stillman had been born into this world a little over twelve years ago, that she had weighed seven pounds, fourteen ounces and had been twenty-one and a half inches long. It also indicated that her mother's name was Abigail Renée Stillman. And that her father's name was Carver Venner.

"Nevertheless," Carver said, "this doesn't prove anything."

"It proves that you're the child's father."

"No, it proves that Abby Stillman filled out a form and *said* that I'm the child's father. Hell, it could have been any number of men. Abby was a great girl and a lot of fun to be around, but she wasn't exactly a one-man woman. I wasn't the only guy she ever dated."

"But you are the one she said is the father of her child."

"That doesn't prove anything," he repeated.

Mostly Harmless Garrett, who was proving to be anything but studied him some more. He was starting to feel like some kind of lab specimen the way she kept staring at him like that. Her eyes were so dark, he could scarcely tell where the brown of her irises ended and the black of her pupils began. Those eyes, like the rest of her, haunted him.

"Nevertheless," she said, taking the birth certificate back from him, "you're the one who's responsible for the girl, now that her mother is dead."

"That's ridiculous," Carver countered. "She's not my daughter."

"What year did you meet Abigail Stillman?" the caseworker asked in an obvious effort to try a different route.

Carver thought for a moment. "Let's see now... I was down in Guatemala working on a story for *Mother Jones* about how American businesses were taking advantage of the local labor. Abby, if I recall, was covering the local elections for UPI. That would have been..." He ticked off the years on both hands, then started over, touching three more fingers. "Almost exactly thirteen years ago."

"So the timing would be about right."

He shook his head. "No, it wouldn't, because you said this kid is twelve, right?"

M. H. Garrett nodded. "Twelve years and three months. Add to that nine months of gestation, and her date of conception would be... almost exactly thirteen years ago."

Carver didn't like that line of reasoning one bit. And it still didn't prove a damned thing. Abby Stillman *had* been a real party girl. She hadn't exactly been promiscuous, but she had liked men. A lot. And there had been plenty of men in Guatemala besides him back then. Any one of them could be this Rachel kid's father. His name on an official document didn't mean anything, and he told the caseworker so.

Unfortunately, M. H. Garrett and the state of Pennsylvania saw things a little differently. "Sorry," she told him, "but as long as you're listed as Rachel Stillman's father on her birth certificate, the law says you're responsible for her now that her mother is dead. Unless you go to court and prove beyond a reasonable doubt that the girl is not your daughter.''

"Then I'll go to court and prove it beyond a reasonable doubt.''

"Fine. In the meantime, just make sure you show up at the airport tomorrow morning at eleven-thirty, a half hour before Rachel's plane arrives. You and I are both going to be there to meet her.''

That said, M. H. Garrett, Caseworker, scooped up her impressive array of documents and stuffed them back into her satchel, snapping the briefcase shut with all the aplomb and confidence of Clarence Darrow. Then she stood and collected her trench coat from the rack by the door and shrugged back into it.

"USAir flight number 422,'' she said as she turned up her collar. "Arrives at 12:04 p.m. Be there, Mr. Venner, or risk the wrath of the Child Welfare Office.''

He chuckled, a derisive sound completely lacking in mirth. "Oh, and I'm supposed to be terrified of a bunch of overextended social workers who don't even have the time or organization to tell me I've become a father.''

At his assertion, M. H. Garrett slouched a little, looking even more tired than Carver felt. "Yeah,'' she said. "You're supposed to be terrified of us. Maybe we're overextended, disorganized and pressed for time, but at least we care about our kids. And maybe we don't always get the job done right, but we do our best.''

She reached behind herself for the doorknob and pulled the door open, but her gaze never left his. "I've been assigned to your case, Mr. Venner, and I'm going to do my best to make sure that you and your daughter get situated properly. If you need counseling, I'll arrange it. If you need financial assistance, I'll see what I can do. If you need help getting her enrolled in school, I'll take care of it.''

"And if I need the services of a lawyer to prove this is all just a scam?'' he asked pointedly.

"Then you're on your own. Although I do have legal counsel at my disposal, I'll only notify them if you don't show up at the airport tomorrow or if you conveniently decide to leave town. Like I said, I'll do what I can for you and the girl. Because as far as I'm concerned, and as far as the law is concerned, Rachel Stillman is your daughter."

He was about to object again when he decided it would probably be fruitless to do so. He knew a good lawyer, one who'd pulled his butt out of a sling on more than one occasion. This Rachel Stillman thing would be a piece of cake for her. Before the kid's plane hit the runway, Carver would be off the hook.

He watched M. H. Garrett's back as she descended the stairs, still rattling his brain trying to remember where he knew her from. He even stepped out into the hallway to lean over the banister, and continued to observe her until her dark head disappeared into the stairwell completely.

Only when she was safely out of sight did it finally strike Carver in a burst of memory where he had met her. And once he remembered, he immediately recalled what the M.H. stood for. It didn't stand for *Mostly Harmless*. It stood for Madelaine Helena. He also recalled that although Maddy was a lot of things, as far as he was concerned, *harmless* wasn't one of them.

Madelaine Garrett settled herself wearily into the driver's seat of her aged sedan and sighed. She told herself she should be worrying about the outcome of the Stillman case. Or about the outcome of any number of cases assigned to her docket. She told herself she should be studying the ragged city map in her glove compartment to locate the address of the next family she had to visit that day. She told herself she should even be thinking about what she was going to do for lunch, since she hadn't consumed anything but coffee for more than seven hours. Instead, only one thought meandered through her brain.

Carver Venner hadn't remembered her. He hadn't recognized her at all.

Uncertain whether she was happy or sad about the realization, she angled the rearview mirror down toward herself and studied her reflection. Had she really changed that much since she had last seen him? Her face was still oval shaped, and her fair skin was still almost too pale. Her eyes were still brown and her hair was still black, albeit significantly touched with gray and considerably shorter than the waist-length tresses she had sported twenty years ago. The glasses she wore now weren't so very different from those she had worn throughout high school, but these days they were considered fashionable instead of geeky.

Although she had been a little on the pudgy side as a teenager, she reminded herself. And she had shed all her surplus weight and more while going through her divorce five years ago. She was quite a bit thinner now than she had been as an adolescent—really too thin, she knew—something that made her eyes seem larger and her lips fuller than they had been before, something that more clearly defined what had turned out to be surprisingly stark cheekbones. Maybe that was why Carver hadn't recognized her, she thought.

Or maybe he hadn't recognized her, she pondered further, because she simply wasn't anything at all like the kid he'd known at Strickler High School. Maddy leaned her head back against the seat and inhaled an unsteady breath. Boy, would Carver laugh hysterically if he only knew how right he'd been about so many things.

She turned the key in the ignition and waited for a moment while her little car sputtered to life. It groaned and grated and finally choked itself into gear, and Maddy drove forward with no particular destination in mind.

She had thirty-two cases assigned to her at the moment, not one of which showed any promise of turning out well. When the Rachel Stillman file had landed on her desk, she had at first embraced high hopes for it. Only when she'd realized the man she would be informing of Rachel's existence was Carver Venner had she tried to get someone else to take the case. She'd pleaded with Vivian and Mohammed to pay back favors they owed her, and had even tried to bribe Eric. But, like she, everyone else at Welfare was over-burdened with casework as it was. As usual, no one had the time.

Maddy caught sight of a fast-food chain up ahead and flipped on her right turn signal to make a quick stop at the drive-thru. When she exited with a greasy cheeseburger and fries and diet soda in hand, however, she suddenly lost her appetite. She couldn't remember the last time she'd actually been hungry. Funny, at one time food had been her greatest comforter. Nowadays, even the most decadent confection in the world couldn't ease the feelings of hope-lessness that wanted to drag her down.

She pulled into the parking lot of a downtown Philly church and reached into the glove compartment for her map. Another new case, she thought as she flipped through her binder looking for the name of the family in question. Another lost cause.

She suddenly felt overwhelmed, a feeling she had to bat-tle every minute of the day lately. It was all Carver's fault, she thought. Seeing him again had made her ache for a time in her life when things had been so much simpler, so much happier.

"God, Maddy," she scolded herself as she finally lo-cated the file she'd been seeking. Immediately she ignored it and stared blindly out the window at the passing traffic instead. "If you're thinking of high school as a simpler, happier time, you're definitely getting maudlin in your old age. Not to mention delusional."

Her years at Strickler High School had been neither par-ticularly simple, nor especially happy. The only child of parents who had adored her to the point of sheltering her from everything that might make her unhappy, Maddy Saunders had been the nerdy kid who wore the wrong clothes, listened to the wrong music and read way too many books. She'd been the brainy girl with big glasses, the only one in Chemistry who'd thought logarithms were a piece of cake, the only one in English who'd thought *Lysistrata* was hilarious.

She'd always been the nice kid. The other students, when they'd bothered to think of her at all, had referred to her as "Goody." As in "Goody Two-shoes," as in "Good God, she's so naive." The nickname hadn't bothered Maddy, though. She'd considered it a compliment. Because back then, it had been true. She'd been a good girl with a good mind, good manners and a good heart. And twenty years ago, she'd also been something else she wasn't anymore and would never be again—an optimist. She had always been certain that the world was, in essence, a good place, a place where she could make a difference.

Boy, what a laugh that was, she thought now. Had she ever been that innocent? That naive? That stupid? Everyone else at Strickler High had seemed to think so. Especially Carver Venner. But Carver had differed from the other kids in one respect: where the others had pretty much overlooked and dismissed her, he'd seemed to single her out on a regular basis. He'd teased her relentlessly, infuriated her daily, and generally made a mockery of her decency.

And then there was that episode during the senior play, that kiss behind the cave scenery during Act One of *Macbeth*. Even if it had been brief and passionless, and even if he had only meant it as something else to make her crazy, Carver's kiss had been the first one Maddy had ever received from a boy. As maddening as Carver Venner had been, she'd never been able to forget him because of that.

And now, dammit, he had to come barreling back into her life. When she least expected it, when she was ill-equipped to handle it.

She closed her eyes and remembered again the way he had looked when he'd thrown open his front door. Half naked, with his dark hair falling over his forehead and his unshaven jaw set in exasperation, he'd looked like some brooding gothic hero. So incredibly masculine. An odd thrill of excitement had wound through Maddy unlike anything she'd ever felt. He'd been a wiry kid back in high school, she remembered. Now he was solid rock.

The moment she'd seen him, she'd been nearly overcome by an inexplicable urge to lean against him and feel his arms around her. For some reason she still couldn't figure out, she had wanted to bury her face in his neck and inhale great gulps of him. She'd wanted him to make her feel as strong as he looked. Instead, she hadn't even let him know who she was. Because that would have been a foolish thing to do. That would have made him remember too many things, too.

After her divorce, Maddy had only kept her married name because it would have been too inconvenient and time-consuming to change it back to Saunders. She'd never thought she would have a reason to be thankful she'd kept Dennis Garrett's name, especially since she hadn't been able to keep Dennis. But because she was no longer Maddy Saunders—neither literally not figuratively—there was absolutely no reason for Carver Venner to find out who he was actually dealing with. Her time with him and his daughter would be minimal, then she could slip discreetly out of their lives without a backward glance never to see Carver again.

How very like him to have fathered a child without even knowing it, she thought.

Pushing the memory of Carver away, Madelaine Garrett blew an errant strand of hair out of her eyes, found the street she'd been looking for on the map and lurched her little car back into gear. She didn't have to think about him any more today, she told herself. Tomorrow would be soon enough.

And suddenly, for no good reason she could name—and for the first time in years—Madelaine Garrett was actually looking forward to the following day.

Two

Carver arrived at the airport even earlier than he'd been instructed, but not because he was excited about seeing this kid that the state of Pennsylvania insisted was his daughter. Simply put, he was quite certain she wasn't. He couldn't imagine why Abby Stillman would have tagged him for paternity, but he was convinced there was no way he could be responsible for some kid who'd been running around L.A. for twelve years. The idea that he had been a father for that long—or for any amount of time—without even knowing it was simply too troubling for Carver to consider.

Unfortunately for him, however, according to his lawyer, he was indeed going to have to prove his conviction in a court of law. Still, she'd told him it shouldn't be such a difficult thing to do—a simple DNA test would give the needed evidence. It was only a matter of time before this whole mess was cleared up.

In the meantime, however, Carver had to play by the rules of the Child Welfare Office. Yet even his legal obligation wasn't the real reason he had come to the airport today. No, if he was perfectly honest with himself, he knew the real reason he'd come, the reason he'd even arrived early, was because he was curious about the social worker assigned to his case. The more he'd thought about her since her departure the day before, the more convinced he had become that M. H. Garrett was in fact Maddy Saunders, a girl he'd known way back in high school, when the world was a warmer, happier place.

A girl, he recalled now, who had always driven him nuts.

Maddy Saunders had been the most infuriating human being Carver Venner had ever met, a Pollyanna of obscene proportions. She had been convinced that the world was full of goodness and light and that the media just made things seem bad to make more money. She had been certain that the people who ran the country had nothing but good intentions and only the welfare of the American people at heart. She had thought it was only a matter of time before inflation was whipped, violent crime was crushed, and poverty was overcome. Her self-professed role model had been Mary Poppins.

She had, quite frankly, made Carver sick.

As if roused by his musings, the woman in question came walking down the terminal toward him, her beige tailored skirt skimming just below her knees, her cream-colored shirt nearly obscured by her massive trench coat. She took her time approaching him, as if reluctant to get too close, her battered satchel banging against her calf all the way.

Funny, Carver thought as he contemplated the well-turned legs below the skirt, he'd never noticed before what great gams Maddy Saunders had.

She seemed to slow her pace when she looked up and saw him, something that convinced him even more completely that he'd been right about her identity. As soon as she was close enough for her to hear him, he dipped his head once in her direction and greeted her simply, "Maddy."

She blushed as if she were a four-year-old child caught in her first lie. "So, you, uh, you remember me after all."

He smiled wryly. "You're not exactly someone I could easily forget."

His statement didn't require a comment, and she didn't seem any too willing to offer one. Instead she only stood there looking at him in that unnerving way she had the day before. Little by little, the silence between them stretched and became more disconcerting. And little by little, Carver began to feel the same edginess Maddy Saunders had always roused in him.

"Boy, you sure whacked your hair," he finally said, unable to keep himself from reaching out to tuck a short strand behind her ear. Immediately after completing the action, he dropped his hand back to his side, surprised and unsettled at how easily the gesture had come. Twenty years seemed to dissolve into nothing, and he was suddenly right back at Strickler High, sneaking up on Maddy to tug on the long, black braid that had always beckoned to him.

"I had it cut short a long time ago," she told him as she lifted her own hand to put the strand of hair back where it had been before he touched her. He decided he must have imagined the way her fingers seemed to shake almost imperceptibly as she did so. "It was getting to be too much trouble to take care of. I didn't have the time."

He nodded, letting his gaze wander over the rest of her. "You've dropped a lot of weight, too."

She sighed, as if giving in to what would be an inevitable line of questioning. "Yes. I have."

"You're too skinny."

"I know."

He frowned at her unwillingness to communicate—her unwillingness to spar with him—when that was what the two of them had excelled at in high school. Then he remembered that he'd always had a talent for saying something that would rile her into a state of agitated verbosity. He smiled. "And your name is Garrett now. Finally found some poor bastard to marry you, huh?"

She nodded, then hesitated only a moment before adding, "And divorce me."

Carver's smile fell. "Oh. Sorry. Or...or should I say congratulations?"

She stared him square in the eye as she said, "He left me six years ago for a grad student who was his teaching assistant. I couldn't have been more surprised than I was when I came home one night to find him packing his bag. It just seemed like such a cliché, you know? Sometimes I still have trouble believing it happened."

Carver nodded slowly and bit his lip. Yeah, he'd always known the right thing to say around Maddy, all right. And she'd always been able to make him feel like a total jerk. "I assume, then, that he taught college?"

Maddy almost smiled at his lame attempt to change the subject and cover his gaffe. Almost. "He still does," she said. "Don't worry. I didn't set fire to him while he was sleeping or anything. Dennis is a physics professor at Villanova."

Carver shoved his hands deep into the back pockets of his jeans and tried to think of something to say. For some reason, he suddenly felt very awkward. Not that he hadn't always felt that way around Maddy, but this was a different kind of awkward. He just couldn't quite put his finger on why.

"Figures you'd marry a brain," he finally said.

Maddy did smile at that. A small smile, granted, but it wasn't bad. "Figures you'd never marry at all," she replied.

This time Carver was the one to sigh. "Yeah, well, there never seemed to be time, you know? Or the right woman."

Maddy nodded, but said nothing.

"So you're not Maddy Saunders anymore," he said.

"Not in any way, shape or form," she assured him. Before he could press her to elaborate, she rushed on, "Rachel's plane is going to be about an hour late getting in. You want to go grab some lunch while we wait?"

"Sure. Why not?"

They found their way to a small café and ordered sandwiches and coffee, then passed the time indulged in idle, meaningless chitchat. Hadn't it been great going to college after having been so stifled by high school? Wasn't it amazing how little they'd known back then about what it took to be a grown-up? How could anyone survive in this economy when interest rates kept going sky-high?

"Why did your husband take a powder?"

The words were out of Carver's mouth before he'd even fully formed the question in his brain. He was appalled by his nosiness and lack of discretion. Then again, he reminded himself, he was an investigative reporter. His nosiness and lack of discretion had landed him some pretty great stories, not to mention that Pulitzer. Unfortunately, judging by the expression on Maddy's face, he wasn't about to win any awards for those characteristics today.

She stared at him from over the rim of her mug, her dark eyes revealing nothing of what she might be thinking. She took her time to sip her coffee, then carefully replaced the mug back on the table. Finally she replied, "Why do you ask? I would think you above all people would understand why Maddy Saunders would drive a man away. God knows you spent enough time making me feel like a misfit in high school."

"I'm sorry—I shouldn't have asked," he apologized. "It's really none of my business. I don't know what made me say that." After a moment, he added, "And I'm sorry if I ever made you feel bad when we were at Strickler. I was a dumb kid back then. I never thought about anyone but myself."

She picked carelessly through the remains of her sandwich, most of which, he noted, had been untouched. "You weren't any worse than any of the others," she said softly. "Hell, at least you took the time to notice me."

Carver had never heard Maddy swear in his life. She'd always been way too nice to do something like curse. There were so many things about her that had changed over the years, he marveled. Not only did she look like a completely different person, but she acted differently, too. Maddy Saunders, though very nice, had never been the quiet, reserved type. Now just getting her to talk was becoming a challenge. He could scarcely believe she was the same person he'd known so long ago.

If she noticed his lack of a response, she didn't let on. And in spite of it not being any of his business, she didn't seem unwilling to share the facts of her past with him. She shrugged, sipped her coffee again, and said, "The fact is that Dennis left me for what he considered a very good reason. He wanted kids. I didn't. So he found someone else who did. He and his new wife are expecting their second child in January."

"Maddy, you don't have to—"

"It's no big deal, really."

"Okay. If you say so."

"I say so."

Carver hesitated only a moment before pressing his luck. "It's just that I always remember you saying you wanted to have about ten kids when you got married because the world needed more people like you in it, and—"

"It's no big deal," she repeated, enunciating each word thoroughly, as if he were a child incapable of understanding otherwise.

"Okay, it's no big deal," he relented, still wondering about the source of his sudden, unusually intense, curiosity about Maddy.

"Fine. Now that we've got that all cleared up..." She glanced down at her watch and quickly swallowed the last of her coffee. "We should be going," she said pointedly, reaching out to collect the bill.

"I've got that." Carver intercepted, snatching up the scrap of paper before she had a chance to grab it.

"It's no trouble," she assured him. "I'm on an expense account."

"But it's supposedly my kid we're going to meet."

"Carver..."

It was the first time she'd called him by his given name, and hearing Maddy say it again after so many years, in exactly the same, exasperated way she had in high school whenever he was giving her a hard time about something, made him smile. "I've got it," he said again. "My treat."

She smiled, too, and shook her head. "Being around you has never been a treat."

His smile broadened. "Oh, come on, Maddy, admit it. You had a huge crush on me back in high school."

He thought he saw a soft pink stain creep into her cheeks at his allegation, but he wasn't sure.

"That's ridiculous," she assured him. "Why would I want to have anything to do with an overbearing, cynical, sarcastic egomaniac like you? Besides, you were always too thin."

He patted his belly. "Yeah, I can't believe I only weighed 150 when I graduated from high school. Age has added about thirty pounds to this carcass."

And all of it exquisitely arranged and proportioned, Maddy thought as Carver turned to make his way toward the cashier. Funny, she'd never noticed what a nice tush he had. She felt her face flame and covered her cheeks with her cool hands before he could see her reaction and sense the waywardness of her thoughts.

Good heavens, what had come over her? Clearly she'd gone too long without any kind of male companionship, she told herself. That could be the only reason for why she was so thoroughly turned on by Carver Venner.

She hadn't been with anyone since her husband, but even before Dennis had expressed his desire to be rid of Maddy, their sexual relationship had been on a steady downhill slide. She supposed, looking back, that there had been plenty of warning signs to let her know what was coming. Dennis had been staying at work later and later, and going in earlier and earlier. He'd usually been too tired to make love, and had always had something else to do on the weekends besides spend time with her. And if she was perfectly honest, she had to admit that she hadn't missed him all that much when he was gone.

They'd stopped talking about anything of significance, their conversations simply stilted exchanges of daily experiences and observations. Her own job had become extremely demanding by then, and she hadn't really had the time to think much about where her personal life was headed.

Still, when her husband had announced his intention to leave, Maddy had been floored. What had been the real shocker, though, was his reason for wanting out. Before they'd married, they'd talked extensively about the subject of children. Dennis had known exactly what he was getting into with her. Back then, he'd assured her that remaining childless wouldn't be a problem. He wanted Maddy, not kids. Bottom line.

But suddenly, finding himself childless in his mid-thirties was a realization he couldn't tolerate. He wanted kids, right away, and Maddy wouldn't provide him with any. So he'd found someone who would. A nice, ripe, enthusiastic twenty-three-year-old who was more than ready to settle down and start a family.

So Maddy had said *sayonara* and wished him well. What else could she have done? The divorce had been as amicable as the two of them could make it under the circumstances. In a lot of ways, she supposed she was still a little numb from the experience. Maybe that was why she hadn't dated anyone since her separation from her husband. Or maybe it was because no one had seemed much interested. Or maybe it was because she just didn't have the time.

Watching Carver Venner as he paid for their lunch and exited the café, however, she realized it wasn't because she didn't have *those* kinds of feelings anymore. The way that man filled out a pair of jeans... As she continued to study him, he turned to look at her, waiting for her to catch up. He pushed up the sleeves of his charcoal sweater to reveal truly phenomenal forearms, then hooked his hands over intriguingly trim hips.

If Carver Venner had indeed gained thirty pounds since graduation, she thought, it was all solid muscle. The belly he had patted only moments ago was as flat as a steam iron. She wondered if the flesh covering it was as hot.

Bad move, Maddy, she told herself. The last thing she needed to be doing was wondering what Carver Venner looked like naked. Maddy Saunders had certainly never done that. Well, not for any length of time anyway. And none too accurately, either, since the high-school Maddy had never seen a naked man outside the *Encyclopaedia Britannica*. However, since married life had provided her with some working knowledge of the male anatomy, she could now imagine all too well what kind of equipment Carver was carrying. Boy, could she imagine.

"According to the arrival screen, the plane's on the runway," he said as she exited the café behind him. He looked anxious and agitated and not a little uncertain.

"Something's been bothering me about this thing," he added when she rejoined him. "Beyond the obvious, I mean."

"What's that?"

He began to walk slowly toward the terminal, and Maddy easily fell into step beside him. "How come there's no one contesting this arrangement?" he asked.

"What do you mean?"

"I mean, how come there are no outraged grandparents who are insisting that Rachel should come to live with them? I remember Abby saying she had a sister, so why isn't Rachel's aunt demanding custody? Why is everyone sending the kid off to live with a total stranger, even if the total stranger is perceived to be the kid's father—which I'm not," he added hastily.

This was always the toughest part to explain, Maddy thought. How did one make people like Carver—people who came from loving families—understand that a lot of kids didn't grow up in the same kind of environment?

"Rachel does have a grandmother," she began. "And she has an aunt and uncle. But the grandmother is an alcoholic who's incapable of raising a child. And the aunt and uncle are financially strapped at the moment. Not to mention the fact that none of them, nor any of Rachel's other relatives, has expressed an interest in taking her in."

Carver glanced away, at some point over Maddy's left shoulder. "In other words, nobody wants her."

She nodded. "Unfortunately, that's pretty much the gist of it."

He said nothing in response to her assertion. Instead, he shook a cigarette from a pack that appeared out of nowhere, tucked it between his lips and lit it with a less than steady hand.

"I'll go with you to the terminal," Maddy told him. "But I'll hang back and give you a few minutes alone with your daughter. There will be time for the three of us to talk later."

"She's not my daughter," Carver insisted, inhaling deeply on the cigarette again.

"I guess we'll have to let the courts decide that."

"Regardless of what the courts decide, Maddy, Rachel Stillman is not my daughter."

"Whatever you say, Carver."

"She's *not* my daughter," he repeated adamantly. "She's not."

She was his daughter.

As soon as Carver saw the girl walk into the terminal, he knew without question that she was the fruit of his loins. Her dark brown hair and pale blue eyes, her lanky build and accelerated height, her square face, thin nose and full lips...

Had Carver Venner been born a girl, he would have looked exactly like Rachel Stillman when he was twelve years old. And he probably would have dressed like her, too, he thought. Except that his clothes would have fit. Everything Rachel wore—from her plaid flannel shirt and Pearl Jam T-shirt to her tattered army fatigues—were about four sizes too big for her. Even her boots looked as if she'd pilfered them from a six-foot-plus construction worker.

Her hair hung down around her shoulders with two strands in front wrapped in some kind of multicolored thread, and when she tucked the uncombed tresses behind her ears, he saw that one was pierced approximately a half dozen times, the other even more. Seemingly hundreds of bracelets made of everything from rubber to straw circled her forearms, and a long pendant—a peace symbol almost identical to one he'd worn when he was her age—swung between what would someday be breasts.

She approached him without ever slowing or altering her stride—as if she knew as immediately as he that they were related—eyed him warily, sighed dramatically, cracked her gum a couple of times and said, "I'm not calling you Daddy."

Nonplussed, Carver fired back, "Who asked you to?"

Rachel shrugged, as if she couldn't care less about anything, nodded toward the cigarette burning between his fingers and asked, "Got another smoke?"

He glanced down at his hand, then back at the girl. "What, for you?"

She nodded.

"Are you nuts?"

This time she shook her head.

He sucked hard on the cigarette, and amid a billowing expulsion of smoke asked, "Don't you know these things will kill you?"

She eyed him blandly. "Doesn't seem to worry you too much."

"Yeah, well . . ." Carver looked down at the cigarette, reluctantly tossed it to the floor and ground it out with the toe of his hiking boot. He frowned. "Well, maybe it should worry you."

She made a face, one Carver was certain was endemic of twelve-year-olds everywhere. "Nothing worries me. I'm a kid. Haven't you heard? We're immortal."

Oh, yeah, Carver thought. She was his offspring, all right. Sarcastic, cocky and smart-mouthed as all get out. He suddenly regretted a lot of things he'd said to his own parents when he was a boy.

Without even realizing he needed to sit down, he slumped into a nearby chair. He dropped his head into his hands, raked his fingers through his hair and tried not to panic. A daughter. God. Who knew?

"Mom told me I could get my nose pierced back in L.A., but she, you know, checked out on me before she could sign the permission slip. So, what do you say? You got a problem with it?"

Carver looked up again to find that his daughter—his *daughter*—had taken the seat next to his. She studied him with a steady, to-the-point gaze, apparently completely unburdened of any grief one might have expected her to feel for the loss of the woman who had raised her.

"Checked out on you?" he repeated incredulously. "Your mother is dead, and that's all you have to say about it?"

Rachel rolled her eyes and toddled her head around in the way kids do when they don't want to be bothered with adults who are clearly idiots. "She wasn't exactly June Cleaver, all right? It's hard to miss someone who wasn't, you know, there to begin with."

Carver stared hard at the girl, trying with all his might to be sympathetic. But he could no more remember what it was like to be twelve years old than he could imagine a mother who wasn't around. Ruth Venner had always been there for her kids, no matter what kind of demand they were making. She *had* been June Cleaver, right down to the pearl necklace. And although, thanks to his job, Carver knew a lot more about the world than most people, he still had trouble dealing with the whole neglected kids thing.

"She traveled a lot?" he asked. "Who took care of you?"

Rachel rolled her eyes again, and Carver thought that if she didn't cut it out, they were going to roll to the back of her head and get stuck for good, and then where would she be?

"It's not that Mom wasn't *around*," she said. "It's that she just wasn't *there*. You know?"

For some reason, Carver understood exactly what she meant, and he nodded.

"I mean, they told you how she died, right?" Rachel asked.

He nodded again. "Drunk driver."

"Did they tell you *she* was the drunk driver?"

Carver looked up into clear, matter-of-fact eyes, eyes that held not a clue as to what their owner might be feeling. "No, they didn't tell me that."

"Yeah, well, so now you know."

"I'm sorry," he said, the phrase all that came to mind.

"Look, don't get me wrong," Rachel told him, her gaze dropping to study the toe of her boot. "She wasn't a bad mom. She just wasn't like most moms. She loved me and all that, but I don't think it ever occurred to her that she was the one who was supposed to be responsible." She shrugged philosophically. "I learned to look after myself."

Carver hesitated only a moment before asking, "Do you miss her?"

Rachel shrugged again—a gesture Carver was already beginning to realize meant that she was stalling until she figured out what to say—and stared at her feet some more. "Yeah. I guess so. She was pretty tight. All my friends liked her all right."

"How about you?"

"I liked her, too."

Carver sighed and tilted his head back to study the ceiling. "Yeah, so did I. I'm sorry she's gone."

The two of them sat in silence for some moments, until Rachel finally broke it by asking, "So, are you really my dad?"

Carver turned his head to look at her, to see if there was anything of Abby in her at all. He was shocked to realize he couldn't even remember what the mother of his daughter looked like. But there was a sprinkling of freckles over Rachel's nose, and her eyelashes were impossibly long. He supposed she'd gotten those features from her mother. Everything else about her screamed *Carver Venner*.

"Looks that way," he said after a moment.

"Mom told me you're a journalist, too."

He cocked his head to one side thoughtfully. "What else did your mom tell you about me?"

"Not much. Just that she met you in Guatemala, that you wrote for some left-wing magazine, that you were a great kisser, and that she didn't see any reason why you had to know I was around. She never told me your last name or where you lived."

He expelled a single, humorless chuckle, wondering if Rachel might have tried to look for him if she'd known who and where he was. All he said in reply though, was, "I guess she covered all the important stuff then."

Rachel dropped her gaze to her feet again, tugging on a loose thread that pulled a small hole in her fatigues. "After she died, I found her stash of some of the articles you wrote. You work for that magazine, *Left Bank*, right? The one that's getting sued by the GOP for defamation and slander?"

Carver's brows arched in surprise at they casual way she tossed out the question, as if she understood perfectly what the lawsuit involved. "You seem to know a lot about it."

"Politics were a pretty big deal to my mom. She thought the Republican party was made up of a bunch of fascists who wanted to turn the world around and go back to the way it was in 1951."

Carver smiled to hear such a young kid spout such adult rhetoric. "Well, it is, isn't it?"

Rachel smiled, too. "I don't know. They seem harmless enough to me. Stalling the crime bill that way was a pretty crummy thing to do, though. The gangs in L.A. are incredible. A bunch of pin-striped old guys wouldn't last a minute in some of the neighborhoods I've lived in."

She was way too grown up for a twelve-year-old, Carver thought. She shouldn't even know about things like crime bills and gangs. She should be worrying more about how to get a playing card to make just the right clicking noise when inserted into the spokes of a bicycle wheel. Even during the turbulent sixties, he and other kids like him had managed to hold on to some of their innocence. Nowadays, it seemed, kids had to cash in their innocence early in order to survive.

"You do a lot of stories about foreign countries for the magazine," Rachel continued, stirring Carver from his reverie. "Human rights and stuff."

"I cover a lot of ground, I guess, yeah."

"So that means you're gone a lot of the time."

He nodded. "I'm out of the country a good part of the year. And there are times when I have to do a lot of domestic traveling to research and back up my stories."

Rachel nodded, too. "That's okay. I can look after myself."

"So you've said."

She tilted her head and lifted her chin defiantly, but she still didn't look at Carver. "Well, it's true."

"I believe it."

He wanted to say more, but had no idea how to address a twelve-year-old girl he had just discovered was his daughter. Fortunately, Maddy chose that moment to join them, and cleared her throat discreetly to announce her arrival. Carver smiled his gratitude, then realized she couldn't possibly understand how much she'd just helped him out.

"Uh, Maddy," he said, standing awkwardly. He gestured toward the girl who remained seated. "This is Rachel. My daughter."

Maddy arched her brows inquisitively, but didn't ask what had convinced him to change his mind so quickly and irrevocably. Then she looked down at Rachel, and he could see by her expression that she noted the dramatic resemblance between father and daughter as well as he. She looked back up at Carver and smiled, then turned her attention back to the girl.

"Nice to meet you, Rachel," she said, extending her hand.

Rachel stood, looked at Maddy's hand for a moment as if she didn't understand the gesture being offered, then brushed her own palm against Maddy's. "Hi," she said a little breathlessly. "Are you my new stepmom?"

Maddy bit back the furious denial she felt coming, and tried to tamp down the odd sensation of delight that threatened to spiral out of control at hearing the suggestion. "Uh, no," she said. "I'm Maddy Garrett. I work for the Child Welfare Office of Pennsylvania."

"Oh, the social worker," Rachel said with a knowing nod.

Yeah, the social worker, Maddy thought, squelching a wistful sigh. She supposed that was all she would ever be to anyone. Still, that was something. There were a lot of people out there who needed her, kids who wouldn't stand a chance without her. Unfortunately, thanks to the society and bureaucracy that went along with her work, there were a lot more who fell through the cracks, too, a lot more who were let down.

"Yes, I'm the social worker," Maddy told Rachel, trying to inject a little more fortitude into her voice than she felt. "I'll be helping you and your father out for a little while, to make sure everything runs as smoothly as possible."

She glanced at Carver, and her heart turned over at the look on his face. He was staring at his daughter as if he couldn't quite believe she was real. He looked confused, tired, shocked...and...and kind of proud, she realized. Something in his demeanor told her he wasn't quite as unhappy about this situation as he'd first let on.

"Looks like the two of you are off to a pretty good start," she said.

Rachel turned to look at her father. "So how about the nose piercing thing?" she asked. "You never said for sure."

Maddy, too, turned to Carver, hoping for clarification.

"Rachel wants to get her nose pierced," he explained. "Her mother gave her permission before she died."

"Oh, I see," Maddy replied, although she couldn't see at all why anyone would want to do something like that to herself.

"So, can I?" Rachel asked again.

Carver turned to his daughter, trying not to buckle under what would be his first parental decision. "No," he finally said. "Sorry, kiddo, but I don't think it's a good idea. Maybe when you're eighteen."

"No?" Rachel said as she jumped up from her chair and glared at him.

Even if she was only twelve years old, she was already taller than Maddy, and Carver suddenly felt about as awkward around his daughter as he had around his adolescent nemesis. Rachel's demeanor changed dramatically in a matter of seconds, from a nonchalant preteen to a raging tower of indignation. It was amazing, he thought, the energy that was wreaked by unstable hormones.

"No?" she repeated, her voice rising about ten decibels in that one syllable. "What do you mean, 'No,'?"

Although he was taken aback by the suddenness of her attack, Carver was able to maintain a stoic control. He'd dealt with scary kids before, he reminded himself. Back when he'd spent a week at a New Jersey youth detention center for a story he'd done on juvenile offenders. The trick was to stay calm and never let them know how terrified you were of them, no matter how badly you wanted to bolt.

So Carver turned to look Rachel right in the eye, settled his hands on his hips and calmly repeated, "I mean, 'No. You can't do it.'"

Rachel gaped at him as if he had just slapped her. "I can't do it?" she asked.

He sighed heavily. "That's what I said. You can't do it. Hasn't anyone ever said no to you before?"

Instead of answering his question, Rachel ran an impatient hand through her hair and glared even harder. "Oh, man, I should have known what a bastard you were going to be."

This time Carver was the one to gape. His voice and posture were deceptively calm as he asked, "What was that?"

"I said you're a class-A bastard," Rachel was quick to reply.

Carver blinked once, turned to Maddy for support, then saw that she was as surprised as he by the turn of events. He scrubbed a hand over his face, reminded himself that Rachel was just a kid—a kid who'd recently lost her mother—and tried to remain calm.

"Look," he said, "why don't we just forget you said that and start over. We can go home, get situated—"

"Go home?" Rachel cried. "Home is L.A. I'm not going anywhere with you, you sonofa—"

"Hey!"

Carver's tone of voice was sufficient to stifle the girl's outburst, but she continued to glare daggers at him as she crossed her hands over her chest. She tilted her head back, thrust her chin out and frowned.

"One more blowup like that," he said, "and I'll . . ."

He'd what? he wondered. What did he know about parental ultimatums except for what he'd learned being on the receiving end of them for most of his youthful years? And a quarter century had passed since he was Rachel's age. The world was a completely different place. Kids were different, ultimatums were different. And what the hell did he know about either of them?

"I'm going back to L.A.," Rachel said as he pondered his quandary.

He pinched the bridge of his nose with his thumb and index finger, trying to ward off what promised to be a major headache. "No, you're not," he told her. "You can't."

"The hell I can't. Just watch me. The first opportunity I get, I'm outta here. You're bogus, dude. Just because you had a quickie with my mom doesn't mean anything. I don't care how much you look like me. You're *not* my father. And I don't have to do a damned thing you say."

Carver looked at his daughter again, realizing then that there was a lot more of him in her than met the eye. "Oh, boy," he said under his breath. Then, turning to his other female companion, he added more clearly, "Ever the optimist, aren't you, Maddy? Well, something tells me this isn't going to be quite as easy as you thought."

Three

___

Carver stood outside his bathroom door wearing nothing but a pair of battered blue jeans and rapped loudly for the sixth time. He sighed as he halfheartedly performed the gesture, knowing what the response to his summons would be before Rachel even uttered it.

"Just a minute!" she called out from the other side.

"You've been saying 'Just a minute' for more than half an hour," he called back. "What the he..." He sighed fitfully. "What on earth are you doing in there?"

"Just a minute!"

Carver spun around on his heel and went to the kitchen for another cup of coffee. The clock on the stove reminded him that he should have left for work fifteen minutes ago if he was going to arrive when he normally did, and he hadn't even had a shower yet. Rachel had commandeered his bathroom just as he was reaching for the doorknob himself, shouldering him out of the way with enough force to shove him back against the hallway wall. And she hadn't come out once. He'd heard water run briefly, but had detected not a sound since it shut off. He couldn't imagine what a twelve-year-old girl would need with forty-five minutes in the bathroom. She was only doing it, he was certain, to annoy him.

Annoying him had seemed to be Rachel's favorite pastime since her arrival the day before. On the drive to his apartment, she'd prohibited any opportunity for conversation by snapping on the radio and fiddling incessantly with the dial. When she had finally found a station she deemed appropriate, she had turned the volume up so loudly, it had almost blown out his speakers. And today's music was nothing but garbage, something Carver had taken great pleasure in pointing out to Rachel. Naturally, she had taken exception to his pronouncement, and had assured him he couldn't relate because he was too old.

"Kids," he muttered under his breath as he topped off his coffee.

Upon their arrival at his apartment, Rachel had taken one look at the spare room, had told Carver he had *got* to be kidding, then demanded a couple hundred dollars to do the place up right. She'd unpacked by removing piles of wadded-up clothing from her suitcase and heaving them haphazardly into drawers and onto the closet floor, and had assured him she *never* did her own laundry. And when he'd pressed her about that taking care of herself business, she'd only shrugged in that maddeningly nonchalant way he was quickly coming to hate.

"Damn kids," he mumbled as he sipped his coffee.

Then, last night, just as Carver was settled into bed and on the verge of sleep, she'd cranked up the stereo in the living room until the whole apartment building shook. Within seconds, his phone had been ringing off the hook, virtually every neighbor within a four-block radius calling to complain about the noise. And when he'd gone out to confront his daughter about her nocturnal activities, he'd found her sprawled on the couch with the music blaring, watching television with the sound turned down, a half-smoked cigarette in the ashtray beside her. She had been eating pizza—

the piece Carver had been saving for breakfast the following morning—and washing it down with a beer she'd evidently also swiped from the fridge.

And when Carver had demanded to know what the he...what on earth she thought she was doing, she'd swallowed a mouthful of beer, inhaled deeply on the cigarette and turned the music up louder. Then she'd told him it was what she always did to unwind in the evening.

"Damn unreasonable kids," he grumbled into his coffee.

He was about to make another assault on his bathroom when someone knocked at his front door. There was something familiar about that rapping, he thought as he went to answer it. And something a little ominous, too. Reluctantly, he opened the door and found, not much to his surprise, Maddy Garrett standing on the other side. She'd returned to her masculine form of dressing today, and wore a rumpled gray flannel suit with an equally rumpled white shirt, and scuffed, flat-heeled shoes.

It bothered Carver to see Maddy rumpled and scuffed. She'd been neither in high school. Back then her clothes—although more than a little unstylish and stuffy—had always been as starched and pressed as she was herself. Maddy Saunders wouldn't have been caught dead being rumpled. Maddy Garrett, however, evidently had no such qualms.

"Morning," she said as she brushed past him without waiting for an invitation. Once again, she sounded and looked weary and run–down. "How's it going with Rachel?"

Carver uttered a derisive laugh as he closed the door behind her and hoped he didn't sound too hysterical. "Well, aside from her having some pretty awful personal habits, and aside from her indulging in a remarkably bad diet, and aside from the fact that she's noisy, obnoxious, loud-mouthed, self-centered..."

"Gee, she sounds a lot like her old man," Maddy interjected with a smile.

Carver ignored her jab. "And aside from her having made it impossible for me to answer the call of nature in socially acceptable surroundings," he added, "everything's been just hunky-dory."

As if to illustrate just how perfectly she and Carver were getting along, Rachel chose that moment to emerge from the bathroom, dressed almost exactly as she had been the day before. She crossed to the kitchen and came out with a cup of coffee and a lit cigarette, then slouched into a chair and picked up the TV remote. Without bothering to ask Carver if he was following the story on CNN, she switched the channel to MTV and, as always, pumped up the volume way too loud.

"Rachel," Carver said, his voice laced with exhaustion, "put out the cigarette."

Rachel continued to watch TV, completely ignoring the two adults.

"Rachel," he repeated.

"What?"

"Put out the cigarette."

"Why?"

"Because it's bad for you."

"So?"

"So you shouldn't smoke."

"You do."

"I'm an adult. I'm allowed."

"Mom never minded it."

"Well, I do."

Instead of following Carver's command, Rachel lifted the cigarette to her lips and inhaled deeply, holding the smoke in her lungs for a good ten seconds before expelling it in a series of perfect, wispy white O's.

Carver sighed wearily. "Okay, let's try another one. Rachel, turn down the TV."

Once again, Rachel acted as if Carver and Maddy were nowhere in the room.

"Rachel," he tried again.

"What?"

"Turn down the TV."

"Why?"

"Because it's too loud."

"So?"

"So the neighbors will complain."

"Who cares what other people think?"

"You will, when the police show up at the door."

"Mom never minded it."

"Well, I do."

Rachel picked up the remote control and aimed it at the television, but instead of urging the volume lower, she pushed it up even louder.

Maddy watched the girl with a practiced eye, seeing in Rachel a typical twelve-year-old girl who was crying out for attention, discipline and affection. Obviously she hadn't received enough of any of those things in her previous way of life. Still, Rachel was actually one of the lucky ones, Maddy thought further. Maybe she hadn't gotten everything she'd needed from her mother, but from what Maddy could tell, she hadn't been physically or emotionally mistreated. A lot of kids would love to be in Rachel's position. At least there was some hope for her and her father to build a solid, lasting, loving relationship. It wasn't going to be easy, Maddy knew, but with her help, Rachel and Carver were probably going to be just fine. Eventually.

"Hello, Rachel," she called out in a voice that was the picture of politeness.

"Hey," Rachel replied without looking over.

Carver arched a brow at Maddy in silent question, as if to say, *You're the one who's supposed to know how to handle moody kids. What am I supposed to do with this one?*

With a reassuring smile for him, Maddy turned back to the girl. "Are you ready for our appointment? We should all be leaving soon if we're going to make it on time."

When Rachel said nothing in response, Carver asked, "What appointment?"

Maddy stared at him incredulously. Surely he hadn't forgotten. "At school," she reminded them. "Rachel starts school today, and we have to meet with the principal to finish up the paperwork.''

He looked startled. "I thought you were going to take care of that.''

She shook her head. "No, *we're* going to take care of that.''

"But I have to work today.''

Her mouth dropped open in disbelief. "Work? Aren't you going to take some time off? I'd think with Rachel here—''

"Her presence is irrelevant. I've got a job to do, Maddy. I can't just take time off whenever I want to. I'm in the middle of a story right now.''

"You've also just become a father. I don't know if the Family Leave Act would come into play here, but surely your boss would give you a couple of days off to get acquainted with your newly discovered daughter.''

"Yeah, he probably would,'' Carver conceded. "But I've got people to interview and some legwork to do that won't wait. She said she can take care of herself, and I believe her. Look at her. She's a big girl. She'll be fine.''

Maddy did as he asked and saw a young girl who was sitting stock-still, pretending she was watching television when in fact she was hanging on every word the two of them uttered about her. It was bad enough that they had been talking about Rachel as if she weren't there, without even using her name, as if she were some insignificant nobody. But Carver had also had to make that pointed reference to her presence being irrelevant. If that wasn't enough to make a kid feel unwanted, nothing was.

"Come here,'' Maddy said as she gripped Carver's arm with strong fingers and tugged hard. "We have to have a little chat. In private.''

Without waiting for his response, she dragged him down the hall, to the room farthest removed from the living room. Belatedly, she realized it was his bedroom. Belatedly, she realized that he was only half dressed. And belatedly, she realized just how warm and solid the flesh beneath her fingertips felt. She tried to tamp down the errant images of sexual opportunity that paraded into the forefront of her brain. Enough was enough, she told herself. Rachel was the one who was of Maddy's utmost concern here. She had to stop all this ridiculous, adolescent fantasizing about Carver.

"Ow, Maddy, let go. You're hurting me."

He tried to tug his arm free of her grasp, but she only squeezed harder, telling herself the action was a result of her anger and nothing more. When she finally did release him, she spun around quickly with a barely suppressed, "Don't tempt me."

"What?" Carver asked. "What did I do?"

She lifted a hand to her forehead, sighed heavily and began, "Look. Your life is never again going to be what it was before Rachel entered the picture. Just accept that now and learn to live with it."

Carver negligently rubbed his arm and met her gaze. "Hey, just because Rachel is here doesn't mean I have to—"

"Yes, it does," she insisted before he even finished his statement. "Whatever it was you were about to say, it's going to have to change now."

"Why?"

"Because it's not just you anymore, Carver. So you can't go on doing things as if the only repercussions of your actions will be on you. Rachel is your daughter. And it doesn't matter if she's been around for twelve years without your knowing it. It doesn't matter if you weren't there to change her diapers or witness her first steps or send her off on a big yellow bus for her first day of school. She's yours *now*. Regardless of the way you two have come together, you're the only stable thing Rachel has in her life. And don't think she doesn't realize it, too. She's got her eye on you, Carver, and she's taking all her cues from you. *Don't* blow it."

Carver watched her and waited for her tirade to end, then touched his hand to his chest where his cigarettes would normally be. Maddy almost smiled at his nervous reflex. Until he dropped his hand back to his side and glowered at her.

"Are you finished?" he asked.

She thought for a moment. "Not yet."

"Oh, then by all means, do continue berating me."

Maddy bit her lip thoughtfully. "You've never been around kids, have you?"

He rolled his shoulders in what she could only liken to a defensive gesture. "I've been around my sisters' kids."

"Who are how old?"

She could see that he was trying to remember and was realizing much to his chagrin that he didn't know exactly the ages of his nieces and/or nephews. "They're not in school yet," he finally said.

"I remember your family pretty well," she went on. "And if my memory's correct, then I bet your sisters' kids probably have very loving homes."

"Yeah. So?"

"So in my job, I see kids who don't come from very loving homes. At best, they're neglected. At worst..." She sighed and did what she had to do everyday. She tried not to think about it. "At worst, they get hurt. Badly. Rachel out there is one of the lucky ones. I'm working with her because she's got no one else to help her make a transition from one parent she didn't know well to another she doesn't know at all. Unlike most of the kids I see, she has hope, Carver. And that hope is you."

He looked uncomfortable as he asked, "Meaning what?"

This time Maddy was the one to roll her shoulders, trying to work out a knot of tension that seemed to overcome her every time she was in close quarters with Carver. Finally, she clarified, "Meaning you can't be the focus of your life anymore. Rachel has to be."

He seemed to think about what she said, then nodded curtly. Maddy suspected her admonition still hadn't quite set in, but it wouldn't be long before he realized the truth in it. Despite their history of antagonism, she was willing to admit that when all was said and done, Carver Venner was a decent guy. Once he fully understood what was required of him in his newfound status as parent, he'd do the right thing by Rachel. Maddy was certain of it.

"So what time is this appointment at school?" he asked.

She glanced at her watch. "We need to be there in half an hour."

He rubbed a hand over his dark, rough jaw. "I'm going to need a little time. I have to call the magazine and tell them I need some time off. And I haven't showered or shaved yet."

Maddy was about to suggest that he go to the meeting as he was, seeing as how he looked just fine to her—all sleep-rumpled and bedroom-eyed, with that warm, well-toned flesh just begging her to reach out and . . .

She squeezed her eyes shut and squelched the notion altogether. Carver Venner may be a decent guy, but that didn't mean it was okay for her to have indecent thoughts about him. He wasn't her type, he wasn't the forever-after kind, he wasn't for her. Period.

"I can call the school and tell them we'll be a little late," she offered.

He smiled, and she was certain then that she'd never seen another man anywhere near as handsome as Carver. "Great," he said as he backed out of the room. "I just need fifteen minutes."

Maddy could think of a few things that would only take fifteen minutes, and was surprised to discover that getting ready for an appointment at a high school never played into the picture at all. When she passed by the bathroom on her way to the living room, she heard the shower kick on, and she fought the urge to linger in the hallway until Carver reemerged dripping wet and steamy.

Rachel, she reminded herself. She was Rachel's advocate, not Carver's love. It would be best if she didn't forget that.

She blew an errant strand of hair out of her eyes and continued down the hallway. Rachel still lay sprawled on the sofa watching television, but she'd turned down the volume and stubbed out the cigarette. It was a good sign,

Maddy decided. She wanted to see Carver and his daughter get off on the right foot, and not just for the obvious reasons.

Because as soon as the two of them were getting along well enough to be left alone, the sooner Maddy could do just that—leave them alone. And although Rachel was her top priority in this case, she couldn't ignore Carver. Which, of course, was the main problem. One thing about her hadn't changed in twenty years, she realized. Carver Venner still agitated her to no end.

And now that she was a grown-up, she understood why. It wasn't because he had always teased her in high school until she felt like a fool. It was because she'd been profoundly attracted to him until she felt like a fool. When she was seventeen, she hadn't much understood her own sexuality and naturally hadn't acted on it. At thirty-seven, she understood it all too well. Unfortunately, Carver was no more interested in her sexually now than he had been then. And the last thing Maddy needed was to feel foolish again after all these years.

Nope, it would be best if she could just wind things up with the Stillman case as soon as possible. Then maybe she could get on with her life.

She just had to remember not to think about how lonely and tiresome that life had lately become.

Carver watched Rachel leave the principal's office with a mixture of worry, pride and nausea. It was his daughter's first day of school, as far as he was concerned. And the realization did funny things to his insides. Rachel had been around for twelve years—*twelve years,* he marveled—doing whatever it was girls do while they're growing up, and Carver had been there to witness none of it. Yet from here on out, he was going to be responsible for whatever happened to her every single day.

Rachel Stillman was the most frightening, infuriating, confounding person he had ever met. She was a product of his own genetic makeup, yet a virtual stranger. Although he prided himself on being the kind of man who knew women well—he had two sisters, after all—he hadn't a clue what to do with a girl. Because of Rachel, he would have to play a role for the rest of his life—*the rest of his life,* he reminded himself—that he'd neither wanted nor planned to undertake: the role of father. All in all, he felt pretty overwhelmed by everything that had happened in the last forty-eight hours. And suddenly, all he wanted was someone to talk to.

"You free for breakfast?" he asked Maddy, who had been sitting beside him in the principal's office.

When he didn't receive a reply, Carver turned in his chair to discover the reason for that was because Maddy was no longer there. He stood and looked around, as uncomfortable in this principal's office today as he had been more than twenty years ago in a different principal's office, where he'd been sitting for considerably different reasons. Not wanting to linger any longer than he had to, Carver hurried out of the room. He caught sight of Maddy as she was rushing through the school lobby toward the front doors, her trench coat flapping about her calves as she fled. Without hesitating, he rushed after her.

Outside, the crisp, mid-October wind assailed him, at once sweet and bitter with the fragrance of trees that were bursting with red and gold. The lingering traces of smoke from a distant chimney filled his nostrils and stung his eyes, and the rustle of hundreds of adolescent feet shuffling through dry brown leaves sounded louder than it should somehow. Carver shoved his arms through the sleeves of his leather bomber jacket, tugged the zipper halfway up over his oatmeal-colored sweater and ran after Maddy. He couldn't help thinking that this whole episode couldn't be happening during a more symbolic season than autumn.

"Maddy!" he called after her as she approached her car, parked at the curb.

Either she didn't hear him or pretended not to—more likely the latter, Carver thought—because she had turned her key in the driver's side lock and was about to slip inside when he finally caught up with her.

"Hey," he said as he cupped his hand over her shoulder. "Where are you off to in such a rush?"

Maybe Maddy hadn't heard him calling out to her, after all, Carver thought when she jerked around to look at him with wide eyes. What other reason could there be for her to start under his touch that way?

"Carver," she said, his name emerging from her lips on a foggy sigh.

"Didn't you hear me calling you?"

"No, I—"

She hesitated, two bright spots of color staining her cheeks, and he knew she had indeed heard him shouting her name but had deliberately chosen to ignore him. Maddy had always been a lousy liar, he recalled. Evidently that, at least, hadn't changed.

Instead of calling her on it, though, Carver only took a step away from her and said, "Now that Rachel is occupied elsewhere for a few hours, I was wondering if you were free for breakfast."

Maddy glanced down at her watch pointedly before telling him, "Gee, Carver, I can't. I'm sorry. I have about a dozen cases I need to visit today."

He'd been around long enough to recognize a brush-off when he heard one, and usually, hearing one didn't bother him much. Maddy's, however, struck him somewhere deep in his gut, wrenching a staggering disappointment from him like none he'd ever felt before. Normally, if a woman wasn't interested, Carver took the hint and went his merry way. Somehow, with Maddy, though, he couldn't quite let things drop that easily. Maybe because, with Maddy, he didn't want them to drop.

"But aren't I one of your cases, too?" he asked.

She bit her lip. "Well, technically, *Rachel* is my case, not you."

"Please, Maddy." Suddenly feeling restless, he shoved his hands deep into his pockets and sighed. "This is all so new to me. Everything feels so weird. I need to talk to someone."

He could tell she wanted to object again, and that she was relenting against her better judgement when she said, "All right. I guess I can break for about half an hour. But just half an hour."

He smiled. "Thanks. I appreciate it."

In spite of his recognized need to talk, Carver suddenly had no idea what to say. All he could do was look at Maddy, and marvel again at the changes twenty years had wrought. Had he not been forced into prolonged, face-to-face contact with her, he never would have been able to recognize her. Yet the physical changes of age weren't what he noticed the most about her, nor were they what caused him distress. On the contrary, Maddy had aged considerably well. The tiny lines around her eyes and the streaks of silver in her hair suited her somehow. She was even more attractive as a woman than she had been as a girl.

No, it was the weariness in Maddy's eyes, her slumped posture, the general aura of hopelessness that surrounded her—those were the things Carver noted most. And those were the things that troubled him. He couldn't help but wonder if twenty years had wreaked the same kind of changes in himself.

"So, what did you have in mind?" she asked when he continued to study her in silence.

He had forgotten what he'd asked her and replied with a puzzled, "What?"

"Breakfast," she clarified. "Where do you want to go?"

He gestured over his shoulder. "There's a great bakery right around the corner. What say I spring for coffee and bagels?"

She smiled, the first real smile Carver had seen from Maddy since their encounter two days before. He was amazed by the way the simple gesture warmed her features. "I think I'd rather have a raspberry jelly-filled doughnut," she told him.

He smiled back. "Never could resist sweets, could you?"

Which is why I could never resist you, Maddy thought. Funny, though, how she hadn't had an appetite for much of anything, sweet or otherwise, until that moment. But looking at Carver, with the backdrop of burnished autumn trees behind him, his cheeks stained red by the crisp air, his hair ruffled affectionately by the fingers of a brisk wind, she suddenly felt ravenous. Unfortunately, she was beginning to realize that her hunger at the moment was for something a lot more substantial than food. And it was a hunger she simply could not afford to feed.

Nevertheless, she echoed, "No, I never could resist sweets."

Carver crooked his elbow at his side, silently encouraging Maddy to take it, and without a thought otherwise, she looped her arm through his. It was the first real physical contact she'd had with him in twenty years, and the moment she wrapped her fingers around his solid upper arm, she felt a familiar tingle of delight she'd nearly forgotten. She had to fight the impulse to lean into him and settle her head against his shoulder. Where the erratic desire to perform such a gesture came from, she couldn't possibly understand. It was something people only did when they cared for each other.

Then she forced herself to be honest. Two decades had changed nearly everything about her, she thought. But there was one thing, she supposed, that would always remain the same. Amid all the frustration and aggravation he caused her, she would always have affectionate feelings for Carver Venner. The realization should have alarmed her. But somehow, she felt comforted by it instead. And then she pushed the thought away, thinking it might be best if she just left such ideas in the past where they belonged.

True to his word, Carver footed the bill for coffee and doughnuts, and the two of them sat outside the bakery to enjoy the cool morning and watch the people hurrying by. Maddy circled her bare hands around the foam cup and held her coffee close to her lips, inhaling the warm, damp fragrance of the strong brew before tasting it. When she looked up, Carver was watching her, as if he'd been completely focused on her since they had sat down. A coil of something hot and heavy wound to nearly bursting in her midsection, and she assured herself the reaction was simply a result of the heat of the coffee chasing away the chill of the morning. Nothing more than that.

In an effort to dispel her wildly errant thoughts, Maddy reminded herself that Carver was the one who was supposed to be confused here, not her. She sipped her coffee again, then asked him, "So the prospect of becoming a father so late in life has you running scared, has it?"

He didn't answer her right away. He simply stared down into his own coffee cup and shrugged. "It's just a shock, you know?" he finally replied. "It's as if the last twelve years of my life have been a complete sham. Things should have been different. They *could* have been different. If Abby had told me she was pregnant, that I was the father..." He let his voice trail off without completing the thought.

"What if she had?"

"I don't know. I just can't help thinking that things would be a whole lot different than they are."

She studied him thoughtfully for a moment, then decided to play devil's advocate. "Different for whom? You? Rachel? Abby? In what way?"

Again, Carver shrugged and stared silently into his coffee.

So Maddy continued with her interrogation, hoping it might make him realize that there were some things that were simply beyond a person's control.

"Would you have married Rachel's mother?" she asked softly. "And if you had, under those circumstances, do you honestly think the two of you would still be married? Would Rachel really be any different as a child of divorce than she is now? Especially if she realized that the only reason her parents had come together in the first place was not because they loved each other, but because of a social stigma attached to her birth?"

"I don't know," he repeated. "But maybe if I'd known about Rachel—even if I didn't marry Abby—at least I could have been a part of my daughter's life in some way."

"How?" Maddy persisted. "You would have lived on the other side of the country. You still would have been traveling extensively for your job. Even with the best of intentions, Carver, Rachel would have wound up a neglected kid. And with her mother being the kind of person that she was, Abby still would have wound up dead. At least this way, you and Rachel have a chance for a new beginning with a clean slate. She can't resent you for not being there when you didn't know about her in the first place."

Carver met her gaze levelly with a smile that was in no way happy. "Oh, can't she?"

Maddy relented. "Okay, she can resent you a lot. But deep down, eventually, she's going to have to face the fact that the reason for your absence from her life wasn't because you didn't care about her. It was because you didn't know about her. And when she finally comes to terms with everything, that will make all the difference in the world."

She reached across the table and covered his hand with hers. "Just try not to think about the past twelve years. There's absolutely nothing you can do now to change them. Focus on the present instead. Focus on the future."

Carver looked at the hand covering his, noting the short, unpainted fingernails and the complete lack of jewelry. No-nonsense hands, he thought. No-nonsense woman. How often had Maddy's straightforwardness bothered him in high school? How often had he wanted to do something—anything—to shake her seemingly unshakable scrupulousness? Every day, he remembered. Every day she'd done or said something that had driven him crazy, something that had just made him want to grab her by the shoulders and—

—and kiss her, he recalled in a sudden shock of memory. Just like he had that night during the senior play. Just like he wanted to do now.

God, where had *that* come from? he wondered. He must be overwrought with worry for himself and Rachel if he was wondering what it would be like to kiss Maddy now. It had been bad enough that he'd done it once twenty years ago. And only then because he'd been under the influence of out-of-control, adolescent hormones. No way was he going to succumb to such a crazy desire these days. He was an adult now, completely in control of his feelings. And he did *not* want to kiss Maddy Saunders-turned-Garrett. No way, no how, no sir.

If that's so true, a little voice in his head piped up unbidden, *then why does her hand feel so damned good covering yours?*

Because it's freezing out here, he answered himself immediately. *Even a cold fish like Maddy is a welcome buffer against the elements.*

Carver heard the voice start laughing then and tried to tune it out. But deep down, he had to admit that being this close to Maddy again felt good. Very good. Without realizing what he was doing, he turned his hand palm up and linked his fingers with hers.

"I'm going to be needing a lot of help dealing with all this," he said softly.

When he looked up, it was to find that Maddy's expression had become a little anxious. Slowly, deliberately, she unwound her fingers from his and curled them back around her coffee cup. "I can recommend a good family counselor," she said as she lifted the cup to her lips for a slow swallow.

Not one to be put off by subtle dissuasion, Carver pointedly drummed his fingers on the table and persisted, "I don't think I'd feel comfortable talking to a stranger."

But Maddy parried like an expert. "You might be surprised. A lot of people think it's easier to open up about their problems to a stranger than it is to a friend."

"I'm not one of them."

"And I'm not a certified counselor."

"But you are a friend."

Maddy sighed heavily, wanting to contradict him, knowing that she could in all honesty deny that she was Carver's friend. But that would mean admitting that she felt something other than amity for him, something she didn't think she wanted him knowing about.

"All right," she finally relented. "If you feel the need to talk to someone, then it's okay for you to call me."

"I'd rather *see* you."

"I'm very busy."

"But what about me? What about Rachel?"

That was hitting low, she thought. How was she supposed to answer that? "You have my card," she said evasively as she stood. "I wrote my home phone number on the back of it."

If she hadn't known better, Maddy would have almost sworn Carver looked panicky at her unvoiced intent to leave. "It hasn't been half an hour," he said.

"Maybe not. But it's time for me to go."

She glanced down at the raspberry jelly-filled doughnut that sat untouched before her, then turned and began the brief journey to her car without a backward glance. Only when she was seated behind the steering wheel waiting for the engine to warm up did it occur to Maddy that, once again, her appetite had fled as quickly as it had occurred.

That was the thing about appetites, she thought as she threw her car into gear. You just never quite knew where they were going to take you.

Four

"**Y**ou said I could call you if things got rough."

Maddy sighed into her telephone and glanced at the clock on her nightstand. Ten-thirty. For the first time in months, she'd managed to get into bed before midnight, only to have her telephone ring as soon as she'd switched off her lamp. Certain the caller would be a wrong number, she hadn't bothered to turn the light back on when she'd answered. Then Carver's voice at the other end of the line had assailed her through the darkness, sounding as warm and wonderful, as close, as if he'd been lying beside her in bed.

The image had been too troubling for Maddy to consider further, so she had hastily snapped the lamp back on. Her bedroom flooded with light had been anything but welcome relief, however. She'd found herself in surroundings that were quiet and reticent and lonesome. Her bedroom had reminded her too much of herself. And the vacant spot in bed beside her had only seemed to mock her—it was as empty as the rest of her felt.

She rubbed her forehead hard. "Carver, I didn't mean you could call me this late at night."

"Maddy, it's not that late. It's only ten-thirty."

"Which, tonight anyway, is past my bedtime."

There was a momentary pause from the other end of the line before he asked, "You're in bed?"

Too late, Maddy realized her gaffe. Carver Venner was the kind of guy who would make the most out of the situation. And their history together being what it was, he would no doubt use this opportunity to make fun of her. "Yes," she replied obediently, knowing she was setting herself up. "I'm in bed."

"Alone?"

She sighed, still waiting for the punch line. "What business of yours is that?"

Carver sighed back. "Well, obviously if I've interrupted something . . ."

He knew very well he hadn't interrupted something, she thought. She tried not to sound too exasperated as she asked, "You'll what? Call back when I'm through?"

"It's the least I can do," he said impatiently. "But if you'd rather just put the phone down for a few minutes . . ."

Maddy took a deep breath and counted to ten, trying to ignore his implication that anything she might have to do with a man in her bed would encompass a very short length of time. "That won't be necessary," she finally said, striving to be as civil as she could.

"So you're not . . . entertaining a guest?"

"Of course not."

"Well, you don't have to make it sound like that."

"Like what?"

"Like the possibility that you might have a man-friend over is about as likely as the possibility that you have a dead body buried in your backyard."

"And what makes you think I don't have a dead body buried in my backyard?"

As always, what had begun as a harmless conversation between the two of them had escalated into some kind of verbal assault. Maddy couldn't remember a time when their relationship had been any different, nor could she imagine a time when it would ever change. The two of them simply rubbed each other the wrong way. She supposed they just weren't meant to be compatible.

"Maddy—"

"What?"

Silence was the only answer to her question until Carver quietly repeated, "You said I could call you if things got rough."

Finally Maddy relented. "Yes, I did. So things must be getting rough. Otherwise you wouldn't be calling, right?"

Instead of replying definitely one way or the other, Carver said, "Can you come to dinner tomorrow night? I think Rachel and I need a buffer to get things rolling."

"A buffer." Maddy could scarcely imagine anything she'd rather be in the world. A buffer. Between Carver Venner and a twelve-year-old girl. How nice.

"Yeah," he went on, oblivious to her irritation. "She's not exactly the most communicative person I've ever met. In fact, I don't think her vocabulary includes any words that have more than two syllables. I was hoping maybe you could sort of break the ice for us."

A cool draft shuddered across Maddy's bed, and she tugged her blanket up around her more tightly. "Carver, you should really try to be the one to do that. You and Rachel are going to have to face up to this arrangement sooner or later."

"We will. We just need a little help getting started."

Maddy had a million things she had to do the next day. She had a million people to interview, a million phone calls to make, a million places she had to be. She didn't have time to indulge in an idle dinner with Carver Venner and his daughter. Nevertheless, she reminded herself, Rachel Stillman was one of her cases. The girl was, in effect, still something of Maddy's responsibility. Even if Maddy didn't want to spend any more time with Carver than she had to, she couldn't very well turn her back on Carver's daughter. Too many people had done that already.

"What time should I be there?" she asked reluctantly.

He sighed again, a distinctly relieved sound, and said, "How about six?"

"Okay."

"Then you'll come?"

"I'll be there as close to six as I can."

"Thanks, Maddy."

"You're welcome, Carver."

For a moment, neither of them spoke, and Maddy began to grow a little anxious about the awkward silence. Just as she was about to say goodbye and hang up, Carver's voice came over the line again, dark and quiet and dangerously seductive.

"So, Maddy," he began, the words coming out as a long, low, suggestive string of syllables, "you're in bed, huh?"

She paused for only a moment before replying warily, "Yeeeees."

Carver, too, hesitated briefly before continuing, but his voice was touched with humor when he finally asked, "So... what are you wearing?"

Maddy couldn't quite tamp down the smile that tickled her lips. It had been a while since she'd received a call from a heavy breather. And none of those had ever sounded nearly as interesting as Carver Venner. "Me?" she asked coyly, peeking under the covers to contemplate her flannel pajamas and heavy socks. "Oh, just what I normally wear to bed. Super hero underwear, stiletto heels, and a hockey mask."

"Oooo. Sounds kinky."

Her smile broadened. "Yeah, well, I was thinking about you when I got dressed for bed."

"Were you?"

Oops, she thought, too far. Carver sounded distinctly interested now. "Uh, yeah," she stalled, trying to think quickly of something that would defuse the situation. "I was thinking about, um, about how you mooned the faculty at graduation. This outfit just seemed appropriate after that.''

She heard him chuckle at the other end of the line, a sound that was at once enticing, wary and satisfied. ''And were you also thinking about how you were the one to call the cops and report me that day?''

She felt herself flush. ''I—I wasn't the one who called the police.''

''Oh, no? I happen to have it on very good authority that it was in fact you who got my butt thrown in jail overnight. So to speak.''

''It wasn't me,'' she insisted. At least, there was no way Carver could ever *prove* it was her.

''Yeah, right.''

''It wasn't.''

''I wish I could see you now,'' he said, his voice dropping to a dangerous pitch. ''You're the worst liar in the world—you turn beet red. I'd know in a heartbeat whether you were telling the truth.''

When she said nothing to deny his charge, he added, ''Not to mention the fact that I can only imagine how you fill out a pair of super hero underwear.'' She knew he deliberately waited a few seconds before he added, ''Boy, can I imagine.''

Maddy was certain her face was in fact flaming then, but the condition had nothing to do with her blatant dishonesty. Carver was speaking to her as he had only one time before—a lifetime ago when she had been susceptible to things like quietly spoken words and tender touches. Nowadays, she knew better than to think that the things people said and did were necessarily born of the truth.

''Well, stop imagining and go to bed,'' she told him, hoping her voice betrayed nothing of the odd sensation winding its way up and down her spine.

''Okay,'' he said softly. ''I'll go to bed and have sweet dreams. Dreams about you and your—''

''Good night, Carver.''

He hesitated before replying, and Maddy was certain he was smiling. "Good night, Maddy," he finally said.

She dropped the telephone receiver back into its cradle and stared at it for a moment, wondering if she might have dreamed the conversation that had just taken place. For a moment there, Carver had sounded almost as if he meant the infuriating flirting he'd done. Maddy shook her head and switched off her light again. She must be out of her mind if she thought Carver Venner felt affectionately toward her. She'd fallen for that once—for one brief, wild moment, she'd actually believed he cared for her. That night of the senior play, when he'd kissed her so tenderly, she had honestly thought he'd done it because he liked her.

Then he had laughed. Laughed at her as if she were the biggest fool in the world.

Twenty years ago, Maddy supposed she had been. But the foolish girl of seventeen was now an experienced woman of thirty-seven. Too experienced for her own good. Who could play the fool after some of the things she had seen?

She punched up the pillow beneath her head and tried to empty her mind in an effort to invite slumber. But sleep eluded Maddy that night. In its place, she found herself caught up in memories she thought had been banished forever. Memories of a tall, rangy eighteen-year-old boy with callused, careful fingers and a mesmerizing mouth. But it was Maddy Saunders, not Maddy Garrett, Carver had kissed that night. Another person entirely.

Maddy tossed to her side and squeezed her eyes shut tight to keep in the tears that wanted out. Dammit, she thought angrily. Someone else was always having a better time than she.

"So, Rachel, how do you like your new school?"

Carver watched Maddy watch Rachel as the girl chewed her food with much vigor while formulating her reply. After a moment, she said, "It's okay, I guess."

Maddy nodded, and Carver felt a knot of tension at the base of his neck ease up a little. A positive statement. That was good. His daughter had made so few of those when the two of them were alone together.

"What subject is going to be your favorite, do you think?" Maddy asked further.

Rachel took another bite of her roast beef and thought some more. "I dunno. History, I guess. The teacher's pretty cool, and I've always liked history. English is okay, too. And I like Math."

Maddy threw Carver a look of surprise. He knew what she was thinking, because it was exactly what he was thinking himself. A kid who actually liked that many subjects in school? A *troubled* kid who actually liked that many subjects in school? He'd had no idea what varied interests his daughter embraced.

"Most kids have problems with Math, but I've always gotten good grades," Rachel continued, oblivious to the riveted interest that the two adults held in her revelations. "It's always been really easy for me. It's like, you have these rules in Math that don't change, no matter what. Everything always works out the way it's supposed to. There's no weird stuff to mess it all up." She chewed thoughtfully for a moment before concluding, "I think it's cool how it always works out."

Carver couldn't help but smile. "I always liked Math, too. And I was always good at it. I got straight A's in school." In math, anyway, he added to himself. No need for Rachel to know all about those C's in everything else.

Rachel glanced over at him, then quickly back down at her plate. "Oh."

And then, silence. That was Rachel's way. First, he would try to get her to open up about something, then he'd have some minor, minor success at getting her interested in talking. Then he'd say something to agree with her or share her enthusiasm for the subject, and then she'd clam up tight. It was a pattern that bothered him greatly.

"Can I be excused?"

Carver's attention snapped to his daughter again. This was a new development. Rachel had never asked to be excused from the table before. Normally, when she was finished eating, she shoved her plate to the middle of the table, rose from her chair without a word and left the kitchen for the living room. There, she would switch on the television, turn it up way too loud, and sit for the remainder of the evening ignoring him.

Her politeness now, he was certain, was for Maddy's benefit and not his own. But whether Rachel had adopted her good manners because she wanted to impress Maddy or because she was fearful any display of rebellion in front of her caseworker would send her packing back to her life in L.A., he wasn't sure. Either way, he supposed, Rachel's good behavior was a good sign. If she was conducting herself courteously because she genuinely wanted to improve her new situation, all the better. And if she was only doing it to keep from being sent back to L.A., then Carver supposed that was all right, too. At least it meant she preferred hashing it out with him in the hopes of something better than going back to what she'd had before.

"Yeah, sure, you can be excused," he told her.

True to form, Rachel shoved her plate to the middle of the table, rose from her chair without a word and left the room. A moment later, the sound of the television blaring from the living room took her place in the kitchen.

"She doesn't seem to be doing too badly," Maddy said softly.

Carver looked over at her, then reached into his shirt pocket for a cigarette and lit it with restless fingers. "She doesn't seem to be doing too well, either," he said through a haze of quickly expelled smoke.

Maddy shrugged. "I don't know. All things considered, with what she's been through—the kind of upbringing she had, the death of her mother, a move to the opposite side of the country that left her without roots or friends..."

He frowned. "In other words, I should be grateful she's not out knocking over banks, is that it?"

She shook her head. "No, Carver. In other words, I'd say her behavior is not unlike any other twelve-year-old girl's would be who found herself in a similar situation."

That wasn't good enough for Carver. There was more to Rachel's reticence than the loss of a loved one and her need for a period of adjustment to get acquainted with her new surroundings. A lot more. She had something against Carver, a personal bone to pick with him that he couldn't for the life of him understand. He hadn't even been a part of her life until recently. How could she hate him so much when he hadn't even been around?

"She's said more tonight with you here than she's said to me in the entire week she's been living with me. Why is that, do you think?"

Maddy studied him in a way that let him know she had no clear answers. "Maybe because she finds this situation as awkward as you do."

This time Carver was the one to shake his head. "Or maybe it's because she hates my guts."

"I think you're wrong about that."

"And I think I'm right."

Once again, they were at odds, Carver thought. Why was it always like that with Maddy? Why couldn't she, just once, try to see things from his point of view? Why did she always have to disagree with him?

"What happens if things don't work out between me and Rachel?" he asked. It was a question that had been dogging him for days, one he wasn't sure he wanted answered.

"Things will work out with you and Rachel," Maddy told him. "They have to."

"But what if they don't?"

Her expression was one of quietly masked outrage. Carver felt certain that if he moved too quickly, Maddy would deck him one right in the kisser. "If you're asking if you can send her back, Carver, the answer is no."

"That's not what I'm asking."

She released her breath slowly. "Then what?"

"Just..." He ran two big hands through his hair and sighed. "What if she and I never come to terms with this thing? What if she never warms up to me or accepts me as her father? What if the two of us are doomed to spar like this for the rest of our lives? What then?"

"I wish I could tell you those things will never happen," she said as he felt himself deflate a little.

She must have picked up on his anguish, because she reached across the table and covered his hand with hers, much as she had done a few mornings before. On that occasion, her hand had been cool and hesitant, in no way reassuring. This time, however, Maddy's hand was warm and soft and comforting. She curled her fingers through his and squeezed hard.

"I can't promise that you and Rachel will have a rosy future where nothing ever goes wrong. But I can tell you that it's been my experience that a lot of situations, given time, do turn out for the better. Not all situations, mind you, but some. And not always perfect, but better. You and Rachel have started off in a situation with infinitely more potential than most of the ones I see. It seems very unlikely to me that the two of you won't work through this eventually and have an acceptable life together."

The words she spoke were so unlike the ones he would normally associate with Maddy. Twenty years ago, she would have chirped at him the most banal clichés about rainbows and silver linings and lemonade. Maddy Saunders would have promised Carver in no uncertain terms that good would win out and everything would be peaches. Maddy Garrett, however, would evidently choke on such reassurances.

He tightened his fingers around hers and met her gaze levelly with his. "You'd better be careful, Maddy," he told her. "People might think you prefer to see the good in a situation."

She almost smiled at him. Almost. Then she dropped her gaze to the table, to their two hands so intimately entwined. "No, that's not likely to be a mistake anyone makes nowadays. Not anyone who knows me, anyway."

She tried to tug her fingers free of his, but Carver only tightened his hold. "I know you."

She continued to avoid his eyes as she said, "No, you don't. You knew Maddy Saunders, a different person entirely."

Once again, she tried to pull her hand from his grasp. And once again, Carver strengthened his hold on her. "So what happened to Maddy Saunders that made her disappear?"

For a moment, he didn't think she was going to answer. She simply sat perfectly still, staring at their hands in complete silence. Then she lifted her gaze to meet his again. Behind her glasses, Carver could see that Maddy's eyes were dark and distressed and very, very serious.

"She didn't disappear," she said softly. "She died."

"How?" he asked quietly.

Maddy's voice, too, was soft when she replied. "Reality. Reality came up and kicked her right in the teeth. She fought it off for a while, but eventually, it got her, anyway—beat the life right out of her. She was just a stupid kid, after all. She never really stood a chance."

With one final yank, Maddy managed to free her fingers from Carver's manacle grip. Immediately, she entwined them with her other hand and held tight. He got the impression she did so to keep herself from reaching out to him again, but where such a bizarre idea came from, he had no idea.

"Maddy, I—"

"I'll help you with the dishes," she interrupted him. "Thanks for dinner. I never would have guessed you'd turn out to be a more than passable cook."

It didn't take a psychic to see that Maddy wanted to change the subject. So Carver let her. For now. But he wasn't about to be fooled by her. She might claim that Maddy Saunders had gone to wear those big rose-colored glasses in the sky, but he still detected a little of her behind Maddy Garrett's round, tortoiseshell frames. True, she

wasn't the girl he'd known her to be twenty years ago. Then
again, who didn't change a great deal over two decades?
Even he didn't embrace the same philosophies that had
carried him through college and into adulthood. Why
should he expect that Maddy would be the same?

Because, dammit, the answer came to him almost immediately. He watched her collect her dishes and carry them to
the sink. Because she was supposed to have been the one to
change the world. Not him. Her. Instead, she had suc-
cumbed to it. Just as everyone else had. Just as he had himself. His realization that she was no longer anxious, nor even
willing, to wield the sword of optimistic hope didn't sit well
with him. He missed the cheerful, nauseating girl he'd loved
to provoke so many years ago. He wanted Maddy Saunders
to come back to him.

"You're going to have to take it upon yourself to make
sure she does that."

Carver's head snapped up at the sound of Maddy's voice,
only to realize she had been speaking for some time and he'd
heard not a word of what she'd said.

"What?"

She poured two cups of coffee and rejoined him at the
table. "Rachel," she clarified. "You're going to have to take
it upon yourself to make sure she feels welcome here. As far
as she's concerned right now, you think of her as an in-
truder, an interloper. You're her host in a way, as well as
being her father. You have to make sure she's comfortable."

Carver stubbed out the cigarette he'd barely smoked and
sipped his coffee, too. "And how do you suggest I do that?"
he asked.

"Spend as much time with her as you can. Take an interest in her. Talk to her. Listen to her. Show her that you care
for her and respect her. Treat her like a human being."

"Sounds easy enough."

Maddy smiled before sipping her coffee. "Except for one
thing," she said as she settled her mug back on the table.

"Which is?"

"Rachel, you may have noticed, is an adolescent."

"So?"

"So nothing, I repeat *nothing,* is ever easy about them. They go out of their way to make things as difficult and unreasonable as possible. For themselves and for everyone around them."

Carver furrowed his brow, puzzled. "Why would they do something like that?"

Maddy smiled again. "It's a hormonal thing."

Carver smiled back. He wasn't sure when the conversation had gone from analyzing Rachel's behavior to investigating Maddy's, but for some reason he was unable to stop himself when he said, "Oh. Sort of like what you've always had for me, right?"

Her gaze dropped immediately toward her coffee mug. "I do not now, nor have I ever had, a *thing,* hormonal or otherwise, for you."

"Sure, Maddy. If you say so."

She rose from the table and retreated to the sink, where she went about stacking and restacking the dirty dishes. Carver was up right after her, following until he stood behind her, his body nearly flush with hers. He had no explanation for his action. He only knew that Maddy suddenly attracted him more fiercely than a stray sock to a washing machine's black hole.

"What are you doing?" she asked, spinning around to look at him.

Bad move, Carver thought. The only thing more intensely alluring than Maddy's backside was Maddy's front side. His gaze fell to her throat, to the long, delicate line of her neck, and her rapidly beating pulse. Her white shirt collar was open, and from his vantage point, he could glimpse just a teasing wisp of the champagne-colored lace that covered her breasts. As he continued to take full advantage of his position, her creamy skin began to grow rosy, and he knew that she was fully aware of how blatantly he was ogling her. But she did nothing to stop him. Which was good. Because Carver had no intention of stopping.

"Carver," she said, her voice scarcely above a whisper. "What are you doing?"

He dropped one hand to her waist, the other to her hip. He started to lean in toward her, inhaling a vague, end-of-the-day trace of her perfume that made him want to bury his head in her neck for a more thorough investigation. "Helping," he replied softly. "Helping you. With the dishes."

"Looks more like you're helping yourself," she retorted as she flattened her palms against his chest to halt his forward motion. "And to a lot more than the dishes."

Carver allowed her to stop him, but only momentarily. Arming himself with his most disarming smile, he bent his head to hers again. "Oh, I don't know, Maddy. I always thought you were a real dish."

This time she pushed him away a little harder. "You always thought I was a real pain in the neck, remember?"

With one final shove, she managed to disengage their bodies once and for all. Carver stood with his hands in front of him, clutching air where only a moment ago he had felt the soft pressure of warm curves beneath his fingertips. Maddy was indeed too skinny, he thought as he had the day he'd seen her at the airport. But he had no doubt that she would still be a real handful.

"You're blushing," he said with a smile, reveling in the telltale patches of red that stained her cheeks.

She spun back around quickly and began to run hot water into the sink. "I am not," she denied.

Carver came up behind her again, but this time he didn't touch her. He only leaned over her shoulder and placed his cheek as close to hers as he dared. "Don't worry," he whispered. "I won't tell anyone there's still a final gasp of breath left in Maddy Saunders. I won't even tell them that you're the one who's keeping her on life support. Your secret's safe with me."

Maddy didn't respond to his charge in any way. She only submerged the dirty plates and glasses and silverware into the sink, rolled up her shirtsleeves, and plunged her hands into the steaming water. Carver could only imagine how painful it must be to have damp heat like that surrounding a person's hands. Then again, he reasoned, there was plenty of damp heat surrounding a certain body part of his own, too. And it was more than a little painful. But it was an oddly enjoyable kind of pain. The kind of pain a person didn't mind very much, because a person knew easing it would be all the more satisfying.

"I'm going to find her, though," he said further, dropping his voice even lower. "Maddy Saunders is still in there—I know she is. And if anyone can bring her back alive, it's me. Just you wait, Maddy Garrett. You'll see."

Her only reply to his pledge was to pick up a dish towel and toss it over her shoulder at him. "Here, make yourself useful," she told him.

"Oh, I will," he assured her. "You'll find full use for me before all this is through. I guarantee it."

As he watched, the red stain in her cheeks grew darker, and Carver knew he'd never seen a more welcome sight. He was right—he knew he was. Contrary to Maddy Garrett's assurances, Maddy Saunders was *not* dead. She was just...lost. Now all he had to do was locate her and help her find her way back again.

Unfortunately, that wasn't going to be as easy as he might think. Because the woman in his kitchen—whoever she was—was doing her damnedest to steadfastly ignore him. She was also trying to pretend he hadn't just had every intention of kissing her, something they both knew wasn't true. And *he* was still trying to figure out that particular development himself.

Things between him and Maddy had never been easy, he reminded himself. And clearly, the two of them had left a lot unfinished when they parted ways at their graduation ceremony twenty years ago. He wasn't sure which fate was responsible for throwing them back together again, and frankly, he didn't care. For some reason, he was just glad to see her again. He would have thought that whatever had been between them back in high school was just some silly, adolescent thing blown all out of proportion. Gradually, though, he was beginning to realize that wasn't true at all. He only wished he could figure out what the devil was going on between them now.

And he wondered just how long Maddy would be around in his life this time for him to get things right.

Five

The gymnasium of Strickler High School in Collingswood, New Jersey was quiet at four-thirty in the afternoon on a Monday, just as it had been when Carver had been a student there twenty years before. He stood in the doorway looking at the expansive room, marveling at how much smaller it seemed now than it had in his youth. He had taken P.E. classes in this gym for four years, had endured countless basketball practices and sweated through scores of basketball games. The gym had always felt comfortable to him. Nowadays, it seemed like an empty, lonely place.

Still smelled the same, though, he thought as he took a few ginger steps forward. Dust and sweat and custodial floor wax. Funny how certain aromas could bring back a wash of memories. The late afternoon sunlight sifting through the dingy windows near the ceiling slanted across the floor in fits, reflecting scuff marks and water stains and bits of stray lint dancing in the air like fairies.

He had no idea what had brought him to South Jersey this afternoon. Under the pretense of visiting his sister and brother-in-law and their kids—who hadn't even been home—Carver had wound up wandering the streets of his old neighborhood, recalling haunts and hideouts he'd nearly forgotten. Ultimately, he'd found himself turning into the parking lot of his old high school. And like a long lost friend, the gymnasium had beckoned to him.

It was the only place at Strickler High that had ever felt comfortable to him. Here, he'd been able to expend all that pent-up energy and unfocused adolescent outrage that had seemed to accompany him throughout his teens. Here, he'd been able to put thoughts on hold and worries out of mind. He recalled vaguely that he'd ended up in the gym after many of his bouts with Maddy Saunders, often shooting baskets until it was nearly dark.

He noted a bag of basketballs near the coach's office on the other side of the room and made his way toward it. The cool, pebbled surface of the ball felt good beneath his fingertips. It had been a while since he'd last played. He shed his jacket and tossed it to the floor, then bounced the ball once...twice...three times. The next thing he knew he was dribbling down the floor, visualizing his layup. The ball swished through the basket easily, and Carver landed on steady feet. It was nice to know that some things, at least, never left you.

"Coach Johnson would skin you alive if he saw you out there in street shoes."

He spun around to find Maddy Saunders—or rather, Maddy Garrett, he quickly amended—standing in the doorway he had come through himself only moments ago. Behind her, the long hallway was dotted with red lockers— lockers that had been beige when the two of them were students—and emptied into the school lobby, which had also been buffed and painted since their graduation. In spite of that, Carver could almost believe twenty years dissolved, and that he was gazing once again upon the seventeen-year-old girl he remembered so fondly.

Then Maddy stepped forward, into the light, and his reverie cleared. She was dressed in a shapeless charcoal suit that was in no way reminiscent of her girlish skirts and blouses. She carried a very adult-looking trench coat and carried her leather briefcase. Her glasses were different and her long hair was gone. Gone, too, was her sparkle of youthful enthusiasm that had once been so blinding.

She had aged and changed as much as he, Carver thought, both physically and psychologically. They would never be able to recapture the trappings of their former selves. A part of him was sorry to realize that. But a part of him found the knowledge oddly promising. Change was good—he'd always thought so. As long as the essence of what he loved remained the same. And their essences, he told himself now, were still intact. What had made them Maddy and Carver twenty years ago continued to define them today. Of that, he was completely certain. He just wished he knew how to assure Maddy as absolutely.

"Yeah, Coach Johnson always wanted to skin me alive for something," he told her with a smile as he danced deftly to the side to retrieve the ball. He tossed it to Maddy, and she caught it capably. "At least hiking boots have rubber soles."

Maddy dribbled the ball a few times, hurled it toward the basket, and missed by a mile. She sighed. "Guess I should just stay off the court altogether," she said with a glance toward her own flat pumps. "I never was good at games anyway."

He wanted to contradict her, but thought better of it. The games Maddy was good at were just of a much more emotional nature. She'd always had Carver's heart in a knot anyway.

"What brings you to our alma mater?" he asked as he darted to collect the ball once again. He realized he was panting as he performed the action, and that a thread of perspiration was trickling between his shoulder blades. Man, he must be getting old if a few simple maneuvers could rob him of his breath and make him break out in a sweat. Then he looked at Maddy again and realized basketball had nothing to do with his breathlessness and rise in body temperature.

"I had an appointment with one of the counselors about one of the students," she said. "I don't have any jurisdiction in South Jersey, but the girl in question used to be a Philly student, and I've developed something of a rapport with her, so I'm usually the one they call when she gets into trouble."

"You get back to Strickler a lot, then."

She shook her head. "Not really. I generally deal with this counselor over the phone. The girl's only been a student here for a few months. I was with her on her first day, to help her get settled, and they called me today because she got into a fight with another girl. I was in the office when I saw you pass by, and I guess I just couldn't resist following you."

She took a few steps toward the bleachers, then spun back around and surveyed their surroundings. "The place has changed a lot, hasn't it?"

He nodded. "Except for the gym. What is it about gymnasiums, that they seem to defy modification?"

She shook her head. "I don't know." Finally, she sat down, once again studying the cavernous room as if she were trying desperately not to study Carver. "It seems smaller, though. The whole place seems smaller. Why is that? I'm no taller now than I was when I graduated. It's bizarre."

He took a few steps to close the distance between them, and dropped onto the bleacher beside her. "I thought the same thing myself when I came in. There's probably some weird physics law at work, here. You were always the brain, Maddy. You explain it to me."

"I can't." Then, after a moment's thought, she suggested, "I suppose it's all a matter of perception."

"Perception changes even when objects don't, is that it?"

She nodded. "Yep. Perception ages even when objects don't, too."

He thought about that for a minute. "That doesn't seem fair, does it?"

She glanced over at him, really looking at him for the first time since their encounter. Her eyes were dark and serious, completely counter to the mild smile she offered him. "Well, I don't know if anyone's ever told you this, Carver, but life does tend to fall into that unfair category in most cases."

"So I've heard."

They sat in companionable silence for some moments, neither seeming to feel as if words were necessary.

"Hey," he recalled suddenly, "do you still listen to Richard and Linda Thompson?"

It was the only thing Maddy and Carver had ever agreed on when they were teenagers, the only thing they'd ever discovered they had in common: the music of Richard and Linda Thompson, an obscure group even in their youth.

"They split up," Maddy said. Her gaze traveled across the room toward the stage and lingered there. "They got divorced a few years back," she said after a moment. "Didn't you hear?"

"Yeah, I know, but they're both still recording separately. Do you still listen to them?"

She shook her head. "No. I tried, but their music is different now. It's not as good as when they were together."

"But it's still good."

She was still staring at the stage on the other side of the room, and he wondered what she was thinking about.

"I know," she finally said softly. "But it's just not the same."

Carver didn't need for her to tell him that. Suddenly, for no reason he could name, he became very angry. He was tired of hearing Maddy spout about the differences that had come over them both in the last two decades. Maybe things had been a little easier when the two of them were in high school, he conceded to himself. Who knows, maybe in a way they had even been better. But if truth be told, Carver had no desire to ever go back to that time again. All in all, his life hadn't been so rotten these last twenty years. He'd had a few laughs, enjoyed some good times and made friends with some interesting people. Yes, there had been a lot of meanness and ugliness during the stretches in between. But sometimes a person had to take the bad with the good, just to make sure he knew the difference.

He jumped up from his seat and pivoted quickly around to face her. "You know, Maddy," he began, not quite successful in keeping his impatience reined in, "change isn't necessarily such a bad thing. Think about how many things are better now than they were fifty years ago. Hell, five years ago, for that matter. Without change, we'd all still be huddling in the dark, unable to even communicate with each other."

Her eyes widened at his vehemence, as if she couldn't understand where his attack was coming from. "I know, but—"

"Things change. People change. Times change. But that doesn't mean the world has to come to an end. It doesn't mean you just lie down and let it run over you."

"Carver, that's not what I—"

"I, for one, am pretty happy with a lot of the changes that have come about. I'm glad that I've grown up. I have a deeper appreciation for things now that I couldn't have had when I was a kid. Maybe my life gets a little rocky sometimes. But getting over the rough spots and playing the breaks usually winds up making me a stronger, more thoughtful person."

She only stared at him when he concluded his tirade, looking as if she had just been thrown into a cell with a lunatic. When she spoke again, her tone of voice, too, was reminiscent of the one a person might use when speaking to an imbecile.

"I didn't mean change was bad," she said softly. "I only meant..." She, too, stood, shrugged into her coat and picked up her briefcase. "I don't know what I meant," she finally said. "Just that...it's not the same, Carver. And it never will be. I don't know if that's good or bad. I just know

it's..." She sighed helplessly. "It's not the same," she finally concluded.

And with that, she turned her back on him and exited the
gym without another word. Carver watched her go, watched
the tails of her coat flap about her ankles, watched her
briefcase bang against her calf. She walked like a woman
with a purpose, though what that purpose might be, he had
no idea. When she had delivered her last words to him,
Maddy had looked confused, as if she had no idea what she
should do or where she should go next.

She hadn't looked like a woman with a purpose, Carver
thought as she disappeared out of view. She'd looked like a
woman who was completely lost. And for the life of him, he
couldn't come up with a single idea that might help her find
her way back.

"Your principal called this morning."

Carver looked at his daughter, seated across from him at
his kitchen table, and frowned. Rachel, however, ignored
him, and instead flipped idly through the pages of the latest issue of *Rolling Stone* that had arrived in that morning's mail—the issue Carver hadn't yet had the chance to
read himself, the issue *he* had planned on flipping through
during dinner, just as he always had before Rachel's arrival.

"Rachel," he repeated, "your principal called this
morning."

"Yeah? So?" she asked, pausing over an article about
REM.

"So he said you ditched school today."

"Yeah. So?"

"Yeah, you know he *said* you ditched school? Or yeah,
you *did* ditch school?"

"I ditched."

"Why?"

"I wanted to go to a movie with Lanette."

"I see."

Rachel had been with Carver for nearly three weeks now, and things between the two of them had improved not at all. When he tried to talk to her, she ignored him. When he tried to take an interest in her activities, she ignored him. When he asked her to help out with the chores around the apartment, she ignored him. And when he suggested the two of them go out for dinner or whatever, she ignored him.

He was making an effort to be a good father. He didn't work nearly as late as he used to and was home by six o'clock a good two or three days a week. He'd stopped bringing home fast food or microwaving boxed meals for dinner as he had before Rachel's arrival, and had in fact actually bought a copy of a cookbook which he had then put to good use. Two vegetables, he reminded himself. He was actually fixing meat with two vegetables every night, *and* a starch of some kind. Okay, so maybe that starch was just a slice of white bread at some meals, but dammit, at least he was making an effort.

And for what? he asked himself now. So that Rachel could come slamming through the front door every day after school and spend the rest of the day frying her brain on MTV. God, if he had to listen to another whiny song about how lost Generation X was, by another whiny group named after a food, he was going to toss his lunch. He was beginning to wish he could ignore Rachel as well as she ignored him.

In fact, she ignored him so well, Carver was beginning to wonder if he existed at all. It was pretty much the way he felt about Maddy lately, too. Since running into her at their old high school a week ago, he had tried to telephone her on a number of occasions, only to end up leaving messages on her answering machine which she had not returned. When he had tried calling her at work, it was only to be told she wasn't in. Now maybe he wasn't the sharpest guy in the world, but even he could sense that Maddy was trying to ditch him.

And now his daughter was ditching school to go to movies, he thought, returning his attention to this latest development in the ongoing saga of parenthood. On one hand, Carver was happy that Rachel had evidently made at least one friend at school, someone she liked well enough to see a movie with her. On the other hand, Rachel had cut class to see this movie. On the other hand, Carver himself had cut class more times than he could remember, for reasons that were even more frivolous than seeing a movie. On the other hand, Rachel didn't have to know that, did she?

"So you ditched school to see a movie," he began again.

"Didn't I just say that?"

He settled his knife and fork on his plate and glared at the girl, who was still too wrapped up in her magazine to notice. He was tired of being ignored by the feminine half of the population. More than that, he was tired of women he cared about treating him as if he mattered as much as carpet lint. Between the two of them, Rachel and Maddy were going to drive his self-esteem right into the ground.

"Boy, you are one surly kid, you know that?" he asked.

Without missing a beat, Rachel retorted, "Comes from having a surly father, I guess. Must run in the family."

"Oh, I think your attitude is more an environmental factor than a genetic one."

She licked the tip of her index finger and turned a page. "If you say so."

Carver bit his tongue to keep from saying what he wanted to say. He reminded himself that behind all her churlishness, Rachel was just a neglected twelve-year-old girl who had recently lost her mother. Her emotions—emotions that were volatile enough to begin with thanks to her age—were probably rubbed raw. The last thing she needed was for some newly discovered father she didn't even know to come down on her for what was, in the scheme of things, not a big deal. It wasn't exactly uncommon or unexpected behavior. Nevertheless, he wanted to make sure she knew that it wasn't acceptable behavior, either.

"Next time you want to see a movie," he told her, priding himself on his steady tone of voice, "go on the week-end. Don't ditch school anymore. Not for any reason. Is that clear?"

"Clear."

Well, that was easy, Carver thought. Maybe a little *too* easy? Why wasn't he quite convinced that everything with Rachel was now peachy keen?

"So, incidentally, how is school going?" he asked, striving for some semblance of what the average American family must do at dinnertime. It occurred to him, too late, that this was a subject they'd covered at their average American dinner with Maddy a couple of weeks before. Then he remembered that the conversation that evening hadn't gone off too badly. And, hey, if something was a successful topic for conversation once, then perhaps one should just stick with that topic.

"It sucks," Rachel told him, turning another page of her magazine.

Carver bit his tongue again. "A couple of weeks ago you told Maddy you liked it okay."

"Then why did you ask me again?"

Good question, Carver thought. "Because I wanted to be sure you still liked it," he said lamely.

Rachel shrugged. "I don't. It sucks."

"I see. And what exactly about it do you think...in what area do you find it lacking?"

Finally, Rachel looked at him. Looked at him as if he were a complete moron, granted. But at least she was acknowledging his presence for a change.

"The whole place is totally bogus," she said. "Nobody has a clue."

"What about your friend, Lanette?"

Rachel rolled her eyes at him, as if he should already know the answer to that question. "Okay, except for Lanette, nobody has a clue."

"You said the other night that you like some of your teachers, some of your classes. You said you were doing well in Math."

She turned her attention back to the magazine before her, once again dismissing Carver entirely. "I lied, okay? I hate it. I hate all of it."

Carver tried again. "Look, Rachel, it's always difficult going to a new school, but if you'll just give it a chance—"

"Oh, like you know all about it, right?" she interrupted. "How many times did you change schools when you were a kid? You probably lived in the same house all your life on some cruddy little tree-lined street in some cruddy little quiet suburb. Your mom probably didn't have anything better to do than stay at home to wipe your nose, and you probably had a stupid dog that followed you everywhere with some stupid name like Bingo."

Carver forced himself to be patient while she completed her assault, once again reminding himself of her mercurial, prepubescent status and her recent maternal loss. When she seemed to be finished with her attack for the moment, he said, "Ralph."

He felt oddly delighted by her utterly confused expression when she looked up at him again. "What?" she asked.

"My dog's name was Ralph. Not Bingo. Ralph."

Her expression soured again. "So what?"

"So I just wanted to set the record straight. And you're right. I was never jerked around as a kid, and I sure as hell didn't find out twelve years into my life about some father who had been a complete stranger to me until then. I can't imagine what this whole thing must be like for you, and I won't insult you by trying to be sympathetic."

She eyed him warily, as if she weren't sure what he was trying to pull over on her. Since he seemed to have her attention, however dubious, Carver decided to make the most of it.

"But you're not the only one who's experiencing a lot of weirdness here," he reminded her. "This has been a little unexpected for me, too, you know. My life's been turned upside down, too."

"Hey, you should have thought about that a long time ago when you were boinking my mom," Rachel told him.

"I didn't ask to be born, you know. You guys could have at least taken some precautions, jeez."

Carver was fast reaching the end of his rope. He wadded up his napkin and threw it down on the table. "Man, you have got some mouth on you. Didn't your mother teach you any manners at all?"

"Why the hell should she?"

"Because you're a human being, that's why."

"Oh, yeah, like you really believe that."

Carver was about to argue further, had even opened his mouth to do so, when what Rachel had said fully registered in his brain. After that, he completely forgot what he had planned to say. Was that the whole problem here? he wondered. That Rachel didn't think he saw her as a human being? Had she thought the same thing of her mother? Did she in fact feel that way about herself?

"Rachel—" he began.

But she cut him off with her most vehement attack yet. "Just what the hell were you and my mom thinking back then?" she shouted at him. "Didn't you have any idea at all what might happen? Didn't you realize Mom might get pregnant? Didn't it occur to you that someone might get born because of your actions? Why didn't you take any precautions? Why didn't you *think?* Why did you cause me to be born?"

With that, Rachel bolted from the table and out of the room. And as Carver rose to his feet and stood nonplussed in the center of his kitchen trying to figure out what had just happened, he heard the front door slam shut behind her.

Six

———

It was after midnight when Carver pulled to a stop in front of Maddy's house in Bryn Mawr, and he wondered again why he had driven there without calling her first. Because he was frantic, that's why, he answered himself immediately. And because for some reason, it just felt natural to turn to Maddy when he needed help. He hesitated before he got out of his car, looking at her house as if maybe the small Cape Cod could explain the changes that had come over the woman he'd known so well as a girl.

In the light of a streetlight at the foot of her driveway, he could tell it was a nice house in spite of its state of disrepair. He knew somehow at once that it was the one Maddy had shared with her husband before her divorce. The homemade landscaping, the uneven brick walkway, the patched roof, the crooked porch light all bespoke a middle class, two-income family that was living just a bit beyond its means. He wondered if Maddy had any trouble making ends meet now that she was on her own. With a little extra money, the house could be a real charmer. The perfect place to raise a family.

He pushed the thought away and got out of his car, making his way to the front door with quick, deliberate strides. He decided not to wonder again why Maddy had chosen not to have children when everything else about her indicated a family was something she'd always wanted. People change, he reminded himself. Hell, just look at him. He'd never wanted kids himself, but now that he had one, he cared enough about his daughter to be out in the middle of the night—when the city was anything but safe—searching desperately to find her. That was what had brought him to Maddy's house. He couldn't tolerate the desolation of looking for Rachel alone.

When Maddy finally opened her front door to Carver's incessantly loud knocking some minutes later, he realized quickly that he'd obviously interrupted something. What precisely that something was, however, he couldn't begin to imagine.

Her hair was a mess, as if she'd been trying to pull it out by the roots. Her glasses were completely absent. Without hesitation, his gaze swept from her head down to her feet. She wore a man's undershirt over men's flannel pajama bottoms and hadn't even bothered with a robe or shoes. The thin cotton of her undershirt molded against her breasts as if she wore nothing at all—he could even see the dark, circular outline of their dusky peaks. The pajama bottoms hung low on her hips, and he realized with no small amount of trepidation that with one gentle tug of the drawstring, he could have them down around her ankles.

He frowned at her apparel. Hell, he could have been anyone standing at her front door. Who did she think she was answering his feverish knocking in such a getup? Didn't she even care about her own safety?

She squinted at him in the dim light, obviously trying to discern his identity without having to go to all the trouble of finding her glasses. Finally she stopped squinting, fell against the doorjamb in an insolent lean, and said, "Carver."

With her pronunciation of that one word, he could tell that she had been drinking. He looked past her into her living room, taking in the wadded up blanket on the couch, the half-eaten pizza in an oily box, and the blender pitcher that contained what appeared to be the remnants of a major margarita. He frowned.

Half drunk and half dressed and opening the door to what could have been some total creepoid hell-bent on hurting someone. This was a woman who saw plenty of total creepoids like that in her line of work, Carver thought. One would think she would take precautions to keep herself safe. Unless, of course, he thought further, more than a little troubled by the realization, getting herself hurt was exactly what she had in mind.

"Can I come in?" he asked, pushing his way past her before she had a chance to reply.

"Sure, come on in," she said unnecessarily as she closed the door behind him. "What's the rush? Where's the fire?"

His gaze dropped to the undershirt again. Maybe Maddy was too skinny on the whole, he thought, but parts of her were quite...extraordinary. "You don't want to know," he said under his breath.

"What?"

"Never mind."

He looked around the cluttered living room again, then gave her another once-over. Maddy Saunders had always been a real clean-freak in high school, fastidious to a fault. Her plaid skirts had always been perfectly pleated, her knee socks had never sagged. And although Carver had never been in the Saunders house when he was young, he'd always known somehow that Maddy's bedroom would be bright and cheery and clean, with nothing, not one scrap of anything, out of place.

"Jeez, Maddy," he said, wrinkling his nose at the acrid aroma of spoiled food, "even *I* put the pizza in the fridge after a couple of hours."

She sighed as she moved slowly across the room, folded the top of the pizza box and shoved it under a pile of newspapers. "Sorry. I fell asleep."

"Looks more like you passed out."

"Whatever."

She flopped onto the couch on her back and threw her arm up over her eyes. "What are you doing here?" she asked.

He eyed her critically, letting his concern for Rachel be replaced for a moment by his concern for the woman who lay on the couch without concern for herself. Ever since Maddy had stumbled back into his life, Carver had been worried about her. She was different these days. A lot different. When he'd known her before, Maddy Saunders had always been too nice, too naive, too idealistic. He'd always thought what she needed most was a good, healthy dose of reality shoved down her throat to make her see how horrible, mean and hateful the world really was. Twenty years ago, Carver had been certain it would be in Maddy's best interest to change.

Now he could see that she had changed. And he didn't like it one bit.

"Maddy?" he asked softly.

"Hmm?" she replied without removing her arm from over her eyes.

"What's going on here?"

She didn't seem to move a muscle, but somehow she tensed up at his question. "What's it look like is going on here?"

"It looks like you're trying to self-destruct."

"Yeah, well..." She sighed heavily, removed her arm long enough to cover her eyes with her hands, then rubbed them hard. When she was finished, she left them balled loosely there and said, "It's none of your business, Carver."

He moved to the sofa and perched on the edge of the cushion near Maddy's hip, then settled his arm along the sofa's back. He wanted to touch her, wanted to brush her hair off of her forehead and pull her hands away from her eyes. He wanted to tug her up into his arms and do nothing more than hold her close. He wanted to chase away the shadows from her eyes, wanted to see some of her old spark, some of her old fire. He wanted . . . God, he wanted to do whatever he could to bring back the old Maddy, the one who had infuriated him so badly, the one who had been his last hope for a world gone mad.

"Maddy," he said again. "What's going on here? What's wrong?"

She still didn't remove her hands from her face as she asked, "What makes you think something is wrong?"

"Oh, gee, I don't know. Maybe the fact that you're lying here in the middle of a messy house, eating crummy food, wearing some guy's cast-off pajamas and underwear, when in high school you couldn't tolerate a speck of dust on your perfectly pressed Peter Pan collars and always carried the basic four in your brown bag. Maybe the fact that back in high school, you were worse than Carrie Nation when it came to denouncing the consumption of alcohol, yet you obviously had a really good drunk going here before you passed out and I interrupted the scene."

He dropped his hands to her bare shoulders, tracing his index fingers down the length of her arms. He felt her shiver beneath his touch, but only threaded his fingers through hers and pulled her hands away from her eyes. Immediately, he was sorry he did. They were red-rimmed and puffy, brimming with tears.

"Maybe because never, no matter how relentlessly and mercilessly I needled you in high school, I never—not even once—saw you cry. But ever since you came back into my life, Maddy, I've felt like all it would take was one little wrong word to make you burst into tears."

She blinked, and the tears he had never seen tumbled from her eyes, falling in two identical slow streams into her hair. "Go away and leave me alone," she said softly, her voice shuddering a little on the final word.

He cupped her jaw in his hand, then skimmed his fingers along her cheek and temple to brush her bangs off her forehead. "Why?" he asked.

She sniffled and blinked again, sending two more tears along the same trail. "Because...because I have a headache."

His fingers came back to her face, tracing the delicate line of her mouth. "It's no wonder, after half a blender of margaritas."

"I mean it, Carver. Go away. I don't want you here tonight."

He crossed his arms over his chest to prevent himself from doing something truly foolish—like pulling Maddy into his arms and kissing her with all the heart and soul he could muster, which he was astonished to realize was precisely what he wanted to do.

"Maybe I don't want to go away," he told her. "Maybe I won't go away. Maybe I think you need someone here with you tonight. Maybe...maybe I need you, too. Did you ever think of that?"

She sat up and slouched forward, dangling her hands between her knees. "What could you possibly need me for?"

Carver was about to list a number of things, all of them very provocative in nature, but the only words that emerged were, "Rachel's missing."

Maddy snapped to attention at that. "What do you mean, she's missing?"

"I mean she's gone. She and I...we had a little disagreement. *Another* little disagreement. She stormed out of the apartment and didn't come back. That was six hours ago. It's after midnight. I'm worried about her. She left without her coat, and as far as I know, she doesn't have any money. I thought maybe you could help me find her. You know kids. You know the city. I thought you might have some idea where she'd go."

Maddy scrubbed her hands over her face, shook her head as if to clear it, and stood. She seemed a little shaky, Carver thought, but not too bad. She seemed perfectly capable of helping him find his daughter.

"Just give me a couple of minutes to get dressed," she said. Then, glancing quickly around, she added, "Where are my glasses?"

Carver noted them immediately on the end table. He picked them up and unfolded them, then settled them on Maddy's nose. For some reason, he wanted to bend down and kiss the tip of that nose when he completed the action. But somehow, he forced himself to resist.

"There," he said. "Now hurry up."

She raced from the room and came back in a matter of minutes rolling up the sleeves on a striped flannel shirt which she then stuffed into her jeans without bothering to unfasten them. She went to the sink and drenched a dish towel with cold water, took off her glasses, then held the wet towel over her face for several seconds. Finally, she donned her glasses again, ran her fingers through her hair to tame the wild tresses as best she could, and told Carver, "Let's go."

"Go where?"

She retrieved her coat from a closet near the front door and shoved her hands into the sleeves. "I know a couple of places we can start, but since Rachel's a stranger to Philadelphia—I'm not sure she'll find her way to any of the usual haunts." She paused with her hand on the doorknob, meeting his gaze levelly. "I hate to say this, Carver, but she could be anywhere."

"Do you think she's safe?"

Maddy shrugged. "I don't know. Probably. She's a smart kid."

"But there are a lot of creeps out there," Carver finished for her.

He could tell Maddy was trying to smile reassuringly, but her expression fell well short of making him feel better. "Yeah, there are a lot of creeps out there," she agreed, only reinforcing his concern.

"Then what are we waiting for?"

She tugged the front door open and preceded him through it. "Who's driving?" she asked.

"I am."

"I'll give you directions, then."

Carver caught up with her in the driveway and curled his fingers fiercely over her shoulder. "Just help me find her, Maddy, that's all I ask."

She turned to face him, covering his hand with hers. "I'll do my best, Carver. But like I said . . ."

He sighed fitfully. "She could be anywhere."

Maddy nodded, then the two of them were off again. And all Carver could do was hope that *anywhere* was someplace warm and dry and safe.

Carver sat silently in a small booth in a tiny downtown Philly diner and stared at the woman sitting across from him. Maddy looked no better now than she had when she had opened her front door to him three hours ago. She still looked as if one wrong move from him would cause her to crumple into a miserable heap at his feet. He tried to tell himself it was because the two of them had had no luck finding Rachel. But in truth, he knew the melancholy that surrounded Maddy stemmed from something that troubled her far more than he and his daughter, and it had been with her for much longer than since the day he had walked back into her life.

"Maddy, what's wrong?" he asked her for perhaps the twentieth time that night.

And for perhaps the twentieth time, she ignored his question. "There's one more place we might try looking," she said instead. "It's a long shot, but there's an old abandoned church on 86th where some of the kids sleep when they're on the streets. Rachel may have found her way there."

Carver nodded. "Okay. Finish up your soup and we'll head out. In the meantime, you can tell me what's bothering you."

She gazed at him blankly. "Rachel's missing, that's what's bothering me."

"I don't doubt that. But even before I showed up at your place tonight, something had you so down that you were acting like a stranger."

She dropped her gaze to the hands she had woven tightly together on the table. "What makes you think I was acting any differently than usual? How do you know I don't spend every night eating pizza and drinking margaritas in my pajamas?"

Carver emitted a rude sound of disbelief. "Please, Maddy, don't insult me. You may have changed a lot since high school, but you haven't changed *that* much."

She jerked her glasses from her face and once again covered her eyes with her hands. "I had a rough day," she said softly.

"What happened?"

Clearly striving for nonchalance and unconcern, Maddy sounded neither when she replied, "Oh, you know. The usual. I left the house without my briefcase, spilled coffee on my favorite shirt, got into a truly spectacular traffic snarl on the Schuylkill, and missed out on a raise because some stupid bureaucrat decided the state's already spending too much money to keep its children safe."

She paused, picked up her glasses, wiped them off with a paper napkin, then settled them back in place. "Oh, yeah. And some kid whose case had finally made it to the top of my workload was beaten to death by his father before I could get around to investigating the complaint."

Carver had been about to finish the last of his hamburger when Maddy's words hit home. His hand stopped halfway to his mouth, and he looked up to find that she was absolutely serious about what she had said.

"What?" he asked, even though he had heard her perfectly.

Her gaze dropped to her hands again. "I never even met him, Carver. All I know is that his name was Kevin Conner, that his P.E. teacher had reported some suspicious marks on his legs and arms, and that I let him down. He's dead because of me. Because I was too busy doing other things to make a fifteen minute call at his house."

Immediately, Carver dropped the remains of his burger onto his plate and reached for Maddy's hand. As soon as he clasped it in his own, however, she jerked it away.

"All I had to do," she said, her voice scarcely above a whisper, "was drive by for a quick interview. I have good instincts, you know? I can usually tell if a situation is potentially dangerous. I've almost always been right about stuff like that. If I'd only—"

Her voice broke off on a sniffle, and Carver could see that she was once again fighting tears. Her shoulders were rigid, and her eyes red and puffy and filled to nearly overflowing. The image of her sitting there, unmoving, silent, coming apart at the seams, roused something inside him he'd never felt before. Carver suddenly felt helpless for the first time in his life. He didn't know what to do, what to say, to keep Maddy from crying. And for some reason, he felt like crying himself.

"Maddy," he finally said, "you know you're not responsible for that boy's death. It's not like you were too busy because you were out playing tennis, for God's sake. It's because you were trying to keep track of a million other kids who might be in danger."

"Fifteen minutes," she repeated. "That's all it would have taken. Dammit, why do people have to do this kind of crap to each other? Why?"

She swiped savagely at her eyes then, and Carver began to feel as if he, too, were coming apart at the seams. He got up and moved to the opposite side of the booth, draping his arm across Maddy's shoulder to pull her close, tucking her head into the hollow of his throat.

"He was only seven years old," she whispered hoarsely. "Seven freaking years old. What kind of person beats a seven-year-old kid to death?"

"I don't know," Carver told her honestly.

"What's worse is that this isn't the first time something like this has happened. I had a case a few years ago where a two-year-old girl was killed by her parents before we could get to her. Just about every social worker at the Welfare Office has had the same kind of experience at least once. It's horrible, Carver. I don't understand any of it."

He hugged her closer and wished he knew what to say.

"I always thought I could make a difference, you know?" she continued. "Back in college, I was so sure that once I got out there into the big, wide world, I'd be able to wreak some changes for the better. I thought I could fix whatever was wrong. I thought people where inherently good. I thought . . ." She inhaled a long, shuddering breath and released it slowly. "I thought I could make a difference," she repeated as she swiped at her eyes again.

Carver eased his hold on her somewhat, setting her away from him only far enough for him to look her in the eye. "I don't know what to say, Maddy. I wish I did, but I don't."

She reached for another napkin and blew her nose indelicately into the rough paper. "How about 'I told you so'?"

"What?"

She rubbed her nose fiercely with the napkin, leaving it as red and swollen as her eyes. "I can't believe it's been three weeks since we met again, and you have yet to gloat and wallow in self-righteousness."

He was genuinely perplexed. "What would I have to gloat about?"

She gaped at him in obvious disbelief. "About how right you were back in high school."

But her clarification helped him not at all. "Right? About what?"

"About everything," she told him. "About the world being a truly horrible place populated by people who don't give a damn about anything or have any desire to make it a better place. About politicians who are more interested in keeping their jobs and their hands in someone else's pocket than they are about making sure their constituents have everything they need. About the insurmountable violence, and ignorance, and hatred and indifference.

"You were right all along, Carver. There's absolutely no hope for this planet. There never was, and there never will be. I can only imagine how you must laugh yourself to sleep at night at the memory of how little Maddy Saunders was stupid enough to think otherwise. It must be great fun for you to see me now."

Way back in the cobwebbed corners of his mind, Carver could remember uttering those words to Maddy almost verbatim. They'd been sitting across from each other at lunch, and she had been talking about some plan she had for the future—a plan that would give jobs to everyone, end hunger and poverty completely and make the world a vast Utopia. He recalled now that he had laughed hysterically in her face as she voiced the particulars of her plan, assuring her it would never work because of the aforementioned violence, ignorance, hatred and indifference that no one, not even Maddy, would ever be able to overcome. He remembered now that he had told her someday she'd see how stupidly naive she was being, and that he wished he could be there to witness her fall. He had thought it would be great fun to watch Maddy Saunders eat her words.

Who would have thought he would get his wish? And who would have thought he would be so sickened by what he had thought would be a wonderfully entertaining show?

He found himself ready to utter the words that would contradict everything Maddy was saying. But how could he contradict her when she was simply putting voice to everything he believed himself?

"Let's get out of here," he finally said. "We'll hit the church on 86th, and if Rachel isn't there, we'll go home and wait for her. She has to come back eventually, right?"

Maddy seemed confused by the sudden change of subject, but she nodded wordlessly and let Carver help her out of the booth. She appeared not to notice as he tossed a handful of bills onto the table to cover the cost of their meal—and then some. Nor did she appear to pay much attention when he shrugged into his jacket and held up her coat for her. She seemed to simply move by automation, slipping her arms into her coat sleeves, walking slowly toward the diner's exit and out into the chilly night air.

All Carver could do was watch helplessly as Maddy tried to come to terms with the intolerable realization that one woman simply wasn't enough to change the workings of a nasty, despicable world. And he couldn't help but wonder why he wasn't taking more delight in the knowledge that he'd been right all along.

Seven

An hour later, Carver fell into a slump on the floor of his living room and settled his head back against the sofa cushion. Without seeing, he stared at the ceiling and wondered where Rachel could have gone. She hadn't been at the church on 86th. And none of the kids who had made it there to spend a night out of the cold had seen any sign of her. Evidently, his daughter had simply disappeared from the face of the planet. Either that, he thought, or she was lying dead in a ditch somewhere. Never before had such a cliché seemed all too possible a reality.

At this point, Carver was literally worried sick about her. His stomach was clenched tighter than a rock, his head felt as if someone had taken a sledgehammer to it, and there was a knot of tension in his neck he wasn't sure would ever loosen. He was certain he had aged ten years in ten hours. Ever since Rachel's arrival in his life, he had begun to feel like a very old man.

The streets of Philadelphia at this time of night weren't safe for anyone—not for a six-foot, 180-pound investigative reporter who'd called the city home for two decades, not for a hard-bitten social worker who'd seen it all in some of the roughest neighborhoods there were, and certainly not for some twelve-year-old girl who didn't even know her way around. Anything, *anything* could be happening to Rachel. Carver was beginning to wish like hell that he'd never met Abby Stillman thirteen years ago.

"I'm sure she's fine," Maddy said, as if she'd been reading his thoughts. She tossed her coat onto the sofa and dropped to the floor to sit beside him. "She lived in a pretty rough neighborhood herself in L.A. Philadelphia couldn't possibly be much worse." She drew her legs toward herself, folded her arms over them, rested her chin on her knees and sighed. "Rachel's a smart kid, Carver. She's not the kind to go looking for trouble."

He uttered a derisive chuckle and covered his eyes with his hands, then sighed. "That's what you think. She's been nothing but trouble since she arrived."

"Only because she wants to make sure you notice her. That's exactly what her disappearance tonight is all about. She's just trying to get your attention."

"It's working."

Maddy smiled in spite of her concern. She took off her glasses, tossed them casually onto the coffee table and rubbed her eyes. "She'll be fine, Carver. Any time now, she'll come breezing through the front door and want to know what all the fuss is about. Then she'll read you the riot act for caring about her and remind you that she can take care of herself. Then you can ground her for a week."

He looked at the front door, as if willing the scene she described to take place. "I can try to ground her, you mean. Something tells me Rachel's going to be a little reluctant to comply. In case you haven't noticed, she's a wild kid. She does crazy stuff."

"Kids are always wild," Maddy told him. "Always. Even you and I did some crazy stuff when we were kids."

''That's certainly true in my case, but I can't remember a single time when Maddy Saunders did anything that strayed from the path of righteousness.''

She looked away as she said, ''Oh, I can remember at least one incident when I did something totally irrational and completely uncalled for. And I've been paying for it ever since.''

Carver eyed her dubiously. ''What could you have possibly ever done that wasn't on the up and up?''

She hesitated for only a moment before responding, ''I kissed you back that night.''

Maddy didn't know why she brought up the subject of that ill-fated kiss out of the blue like that. Somehow, the words just tumbled from her mouth as if she hadn't been able to keep them in. For some reason, her relationship with Carver tonight felt like it did in the old days. Their frantic and fruitless search for Rachel had roused an unspoken intimacy between them that was as unexpected and unexplainable as the one they had shared in high school. She just felt close to him right now. And as a result, she couldn't help but recall that one brief instance when the two of them had actually seemed to care for each other.

Nevertheless, she halfway expected him to reply with a puzzled ''What night?'' She was certain that he had long ago forgotten what had been for her one of the most momentous events of her life. Maddy was about to elaborate, to try to jog his memory, even went so far as to steel herself against the riotous laughter that would no doubt erupt when—and if—he remembered that kiss. She even reached for her glasses, ready to put her mask back in place.

Then she heard him say softly, ''Yeah, you did kiss me back, didn't you? I guess that was kind of crazy.''

She stayed her hand short of making contact with her glasses, then risked a glance over at him, trying not to squint. In spite of her nearsightedness, she could tell he was looking at her in a way he had never looked at her before. The way a man looks at a woman when he wants to get closer than he probably should. But he said nothing more, only watched and waited for her to go on.

"Crazy for me?" she asked, barely able to voice the question. "Or crazy for you?"

He turned and scooted himself back a little, and her heart nearly stopped beating, so stung was she by his withdrawal. Then he lifted his hand to her face, curving his palm over her jaw before strumming his fingertips over her lips. A burst of white-hot fire licked at her insides, burning her to her very core. Seemingly without controlling any of it herself, Maddy felt her eyelids flutter closed, felt her lips part, felt the breath leave her lungs in a quick rush of air.

And when Carver said nothing to explain his actions, she had to ask him, "Why...why did you kiss me that night?"

She opened her eyes to find him gazing at her mouth, his own lips parted in what she could only liken to desire. He shook his head slowly. "I don't know," he said honestly. "I still wonder about that myself. That night you just looked so...so vulnerable, so beautiful, there in the dim light backstage."

She chuckled, striving for a carefree tone of voice that would alleviate the tension that had erupted between them. But carefree was the last thing she felt. "Yeah, I guess the light would have to be pretty dim for me to look beautiful, wouldn't it?"

He shook his head slowly and skimmed his fingers over her lips again. "No, that's not what I meant. I always thought you were beautiful in high school, Maddy."

This time her laughter came out clearly strained. "Oh, right. I bet."

"I did. Maybe I didn't realize it twenty years ago, but these days I'm beginning to understand a lot about how I felt back then. And I think you're beautiful now, too," he added with a smile. "Even if you are too skinny."

Her skin was so soft, Carver thought as he dropped his finger to touch the pulse beating erratically just below her jaw. As soft as it had been that night twenty years ago. He remembered thinking how incongruous it had seemed back then—such soft skin on such a prickly girl. Her hair, too, had been soft and silky then, something else he'd always thought was an enigma about his adolescent nemesis. Until the night he'd kissed her. And then he'd discovered that Maddy Saunders was soft all over. Just as he had that night two decades ago, he brushed his fingers up over her jaw and threaded them through her hair.

Still soft. Still silky. Still Maddy.

Maybe she hadn't changed so much after all. The realization made Carver feel good. Too good, he decided. Suddenly, her presence, her closeness, was giving him all kinds of silly, adolescent ideas.

"That night of the senior play..." he said, keeping his voice as quiet a whisper as his fingers. "I don't know why I kissed you that night. For some reason, it just seemed like the thing to do. Kind of like..."

Instead of completing his statement, he simply shook his head slowly in silent denial of what he was thinking. It wasn't that he wanted to refute the waking realization of the depths of his feelings for Maddy. It was more because he was afraid of the reception he might get from the woman who still confounded his emotions.

"Kind of like what?" she asked him, begging him to put words to the rest of his thought. Her own voice had dropped to a pitch so soft, he almost had to strain to hear her.

Hesitantly, and with much uncertainty, he leaned forward, closing the distance between the two of them until scarcely a wisp of air separated them. He still wasn't sure what he was planning to do. Then he heard himself say softly, "Kind of like now."

He watched as she drew in an unsteady breath, but never saw her exhale it. "What do you mean?" she asked.

Instead of answering her, Carver bent his head toward Maddy's, then touched his lips to hers. He had thought he was only going to kiss her as he had that night backstage twenty years ago. He had thought he was only going to brush his mouth lightly over hers and be done with it. But the moment he felt her melting into him—just as she had so long ago—he knew this kiss wasn't going to be like the one before. Back then he'd had fear on his side—a raw, uncertain adolescent's fear of his own reaction that the eighteen-year-old boy hadn't understood. Back then, Carver's fear had been what made him back away from Maddy.

This time, however, his fear evaporated to be replaced by desire—a raw, hungry man's desire for a woman he'd never quite forgotten. The moment his lips touched hers, he suddenly remembered that he hadn't wanted to stop kissing Maddy twenty years ago. He'd had to force himself to pull out of the embrace and act like it had been nothing at all. He sure as hell wasn't going to make the same mistake now.

He slanted his mouth over hers more fully then, lifting his hands to tangle his fingers in her hair, angling his body so that he could pull her more eagerly into his arms. Maddy clung to him, returning his kisses with a ferocity to rival his own, bunching his sweatshirt in her fists as if she intended to rip the heavy fabric right down the middle. For a long time they tried to consume each other, each taking turns dominating the embrace, until finally, in a searing second of sanity, Maddy pushed Carver away.

Several moments passed before she trusted herself to speak without revealing the tumultuousness of her feelings. All she could do was press the back of her hand to her lips, uncertain whether she was trying to scrub away the sensation of his mouth on hers or preserve the feeling forever. Finally, when she could no longer tolerate the silence burning up the air between them, she whispered, "Don't do this to me again, Carver. Please."

He looked puzzled, even hurt. "Do what?"

"Don't kiss me and then laugh at me, and then walk away as if you'd done nothing more than nod a greeting. Don't make me feel foolish again. And don't make me wonder for the rest of my life what it might have been like if things had been different between the two of us."

"Different in what way?"

She hesitated before speaking, the uncertain seventeen-year-old girl that still dwelled within her moving to the forefront of her brain. After a moment, she forced herself to say, "Different the way it would have been if maybe you had liked me. If maybe you had...had wanted me back then as much as I wanted you."

His expression would have been the same if she had just poked him in the eye with a big stick. "You...you wanted me back then?" he sputtered.

She chuckled a little nervously. "Oh, yeah. I wanted you. Maybe I didn't recognize lust back then when I felt it, but... Trust me—I know it now. And the reason I could never get along with you in high school had nothing to do with our differences of opinion."

Carver smiled at her then. Not the swaggering, arrogant smile of a man who was cocksure of his effect on women— a man who might have winked salaciously and told Maddy he'd known it all along—but a smile of pure, unadulterated delight. Instead of winking and voicing his certainty of her feelings, Carver brushed his bent knuckles lightly over Maddy's cheek and said warily, "Really? You...you really did have a crush on me?"

She nodded helplessly. "Yeah. And you know what's really crazy?"

He shook his head. "Tell me."

"For some reason, I've never quite been able to get over it."

His smile broadened, and he scooted closer. "That's amazing, Maddy. Because the truth of the matter is, as crazy as it sounds, I had a pretty wild crush on you back then, too. I just didn't think you'd ever let me get close enough to do anything about it."

She laughed. "Back then, I probably wouldn't have."

He moved closer still, cupping his warm palm over her nape, pulling her forward until her forehead touched his. His gaze never left hers as he asked, "What would you do now?"

Maddy lifted her hand to Carver's lower lip, skimming the pad of her index finger over the soft contours of his mouth. His eyes fluttered shut, and he expelled a little sound, something primitive and masculine and, oh, so intriguing. This time Maddy was the one to lean forward, her tongue tracing the path that her finger had just forged. She tasted the remnants of coffee, the lingering traces of cigarette smoke, and something else that was uniquely Carver. And suddenly, she wanted to taste more.

Before she had the chance to do so, however, he joined her in the kiss, propelling himself toward her with such zeal, that Maddy felt herself reeling backward and Carver coming in for a landing atop her. With a pair of muffled "oofs," they found themselves sprawled on the floor between the sofa and the coffee table, everything in the world forgotten except for a plethora of twenty-year-old adolescent hormones that had never quite been quelled.

"This is crazy, you know," she said, clamping her arms together behind his neck, still unable to subdue the fear that he might try to pull away from her again. "We have no more business doing this now than we did twenty years ago."

He smiled, then dipped his head to hers and placed a soft, butterfly kiss at her temple. "Says who?"

Says me, she wanted to tell him. Even if Carver wasn't thinking straight at the moment—and she was certain that was the case, that his response to her now was only a result of his being overwrought with worry about his daughter— Maddy was. She was probably thinking straighter now than she ever had before. And she knew what the two of them were doing was insane.

She told herself she was only allowing herself to succumb to Carver because she'd had a pretty miserable day herself. She wanted—needed—to escape from her life for a little while. She needed to forget about the ugly reality she encountered so often in her job. She needed to forget about a seven-year-old boy who had been a casualty of brutality. She needed to forget that she would probably just see more of the same tomorrow.

She needed to forget it all. And what Carver was offering was a perfect escape. He could provide her with a mind-numbing deliverance that would take her to places she'd never visited, places where thinking and remembering weren't necessary. All she'd have to do with him was feel things. Wonderful things. Things she'd never felt before and would never feel again. Maybe the journey would only be temporary, but at least it would feel good. And it had been so long since Maddy had felt good.

"Says who?" she echoed his question. "Says the voice of sanity, that's who."

Carver turned an ear to the silence in the room, then looked at Maddy again. He smiled as he said, "I don't hear a voice of sanity. All I hear is your heart pounding as loudly as mine."

"You know as well as I do that this is crazy," she countered, a part of her still hoping one of them would come to their senses. "We're both exhausted and worried about Rachel. I'm still reeling from what happened to me today. The only reason the two of us are turning to each other now is that—"

"This isn't crazy, Maddy," Carver interrupted her. "This is right. This is something that's been coming for a long, long time, so don't try to tear it down with some half-baked psychoanalysis. Back in high school, we had some vaguely defined feelings for each other that we didn't know what to do with." He bent and kissed her, long and hard and deep. "Now," he added a little breathlessly afterward, "I think we have a couple of good ideas how to proceed."

She swallowed hard. "Oh, I can think of more than a couple."

His smile broadened. "That's good. We should have more than enough to keep us occupied, then."

Before she could comment further, he bent his head again and blazed a trail of damp, openmouthed kisses down her throat. When he encountered her shirt, he shoved it aside to taste her collarbone before dipping even lower. Maddy thought she heard the fabric tear, but before she had a chance to undo her buttons, Carver's hands were there instead, slipping each one free until the well-worn flannel gaped open over her torso. Without pausing to remove her brassiere, he dropped his head to her again, closing his mouth over her lace-covered breast.

For long moments, he suckled her through the gauzy fabric, tugging and laving the swollen peak. She felt his tongue dart out in maddening circles, savoring her as if she were the sweetest bit of confection he'd ever had the pleasure to consume. And just when Maddy thought she would explode with pleasure at his skillful maneuvers, he moved to her other breast to administer them even more masterfully.

Fearful that he would come to his senses and put an end to his sumptuous onslaught, Maddy knotted her fingers in his hair and pulled him closer to her still. When she arched her back, he hooked his fingers into the closure of her bra and unfastened it, shoving the wisp of lace aside.

Only then did either one of them seem to realize what was happening. Carver lifted his head to stare down at a half-naked Maddy, who had curled her fingers possessively and shamelessly in the waistband of his jeans. Both of them were panting and flushed and confused. But instead of covering herself, as she knew she should, Maddy met his gaze levelly, silently daring him to finish what he had begun. Or perhaps it was something she had begun, she thought. At the moment, she couldn't quite remember.

Evidently, Carver decided to let her silence be his guide, because he bent his head toward her again. The feel of his hot, rough jaw, rubbing so fiercely against her tender flesh as he nipped her breast lightly with his teeth, made her gasp out loud. The sound must have alarmed him, because he immediately laved the tender spot with his tongue and pressed a chaste kiss to it. Then he bunched her bare breast in his hand and opened his mouth over her again as if he had every intention of consuming her whole.

He was a leisurely lover, she thought vaguely as he lingered at his task. Evidently, Carver was the kind of man who took his time to make sure he got things right. Even as he continued to lovingly administer to her breasts, she felt his hand dip lower, felt his fingers slide easily beneath the button of her jeans. Quickly, confidently, as if it were the kind of thing he did everyday, he shoved his hand between the heavy denim fabric and the satin of her panties, curving his palm over the agitated, heat-swollen heart of her. Then he proceeded to drive her to madness.

Maddy couldn't remember ever quite feeling the way Carver made her feel. Had she known twenty years ago what such a simple gesture as his could wreak, she would never have tried to alienate him. Now, as his hand and fingers pressed more fully into her, she dropped her own hand over the denim that covered his and encouraged him to venture even lower. Carver followed her instructions to the letter, delving beneath her panties to explore her more completely. Lovingly, leisurely, he traced every one of her contours, then joined himself with her even more intimately.

Maddy gasped again when she felt him slip inside her. The fire that shot threw her was hot, exquisite and nearly unbearable. She flinched involuntarily, trying to jerk Carver's hand away, thinking she must have been mad to ever coax him in the first place. But he only pushed himself in more deeply. And then Maddy couldn't think at all. She roped her arms across his back and pulled him as close as she could. For a long time, she could only shudder against him and waver between hoping his assault on her senses would end and wishing it would go on forever. Then a surge of power coiled tight in her midsection exploded, sending shards of heat spinning throughout her body.

After that, all she could do was go limp beneath him, fearing she would never move again because she would never have the energy to do so. Then she felt her jeans and panties being skimmed down her legs as if borne on wings. Her shirt and bra, too, somehow mysteriously disappeared, and then the feel of the wool carpet abrading her bare back made her finally open her eyes.

What she saw was Carver stretched out beside her, one hand cradling his head, the other tracing idle circles on her naked belly. He was calm but anxious-looking, and still fully dressed.

"I thought you were dead," he said, not quite able to stifle a grin.

She managed to shake her head weakly. "I've never been more alive." She cupped her hands behind his nape and pulled his head down to hers. "Not fair," she whispered. "I'm all undressed, and you've still got clothes on."

He quickly straightened and reached behind himself to bunch a fistful of his sweatshirt in his hand. "Not for long."

"No," she said, clenching fiercely at the hem to tug the garment back in place. "Let me."

Immediately, he let go of his shirt and held his arms out to his sides in a gesture of utter surrender. This time Maddy was the one to smile as she proceeded. Her eyes never left his as she tucked her hands beneath his shirt and flattened her palms over the solid, heated flesh she encountered beneath. The last time she had been this close to Carver, he had been a boy of eighteen, a prancing, uncertain, not yet fully molded bundle of potential. She raked her bent hands up over the length of his torso, tangling her fingers in the springy mat of dark hair, marveling again at how much he had changed.

Carver had more than achieved his potential. He was truly a man fully grown. Maddy had been intimidated by him when he was a boy. She ought to be terrified of him now. But he had been tender and attentive and careful when he'd pleasured her moments ago. He had put her wants and desires before his own, had found gratification in making her feel the way she had. And now, all she wanted was to do for him exactly what he'd just done for her.

"Come down here where I can see you better," she said quietly.

He immediately obeyed her, stretching out alongside her again. He shifted his position long enough for her to tug his shirt up and over his head, then he lay back down on his side. Maddy traced the poetic lines of muscle and sinew on his abdomen with much devotion, glorying in the way his chest expanded and fell as his breathing grew more and more erratic. Finally, she cupped her hand over his shoulder and urged him down, until he was flat on his back on the floor.

Their positions switched, she entwined her legs with his, buried the fingers of one hand briefly in the coils of hair on his chest, then went to work on his blue jeans with the other. She fumbled a little over the buttons as she tried to unfasten them, but Carver only watched her intently and did nothing to come to her aid.

As she worked more furiously at her task, Maddy became aware of a solid ridge of him rising up below the fabric, a development that gave her pause. So instead of delving inside to investigate the promise of masculinity that was Carver Venner, she lingered over the heavy denim casing, cupping him in her hand as fully as she could. Carver groaned and closed his eyes, bending one leg to facilitate her explorations. Back and forth her fingers ventured over him, until he gasped out a plea for her to finish him off.

"Please, Maddy, I'm begging you. End this torture."

She grinned as she unfastened the last of his buttons and pushed his fly open. "End it?" she whispered as she dipped her head low. "But I'm just getting started."

And, as Carver had earlier, she took her time to finish. By the time she did, they were both writhing and impatient and anxious to get on with fully satisfying their desires.

Carver pulled Maddy atop him, her legs straddling his torso, his hands curved over her thighs. Without speaking, he urged his fingers upward, dipping his thumb into her navel as he passed it, strumming her rib cage, pausing to frame her breasts in the L-shaped arc of his thumb and forefinger. All the while, his gaze never left hers, and all the while Maddy's breath quickened to sporadic gasps. Then Carver covered her breasts with his hands, measured them with a gentle squeeze, and raked his thumbs over the rigid tips.

He opened his mouth to speak, but Maddy covered his lips with her hand. "Shh," she told him. "Don't say anything more. Not until it's over."

"But—"

"Shh," she repeated. "Not a word."

"But what about...?"

"Carver..."

But he would not be put off. "Hey, the last time I did something this...this..." He smiled before concluding, "...this spontaneous, this incredibly erotic, I became a father."

Maddy's eyes widened at his reminder, and he hoped he hadn't just blown their chance for a really nice ending to what was becoming the best night of his life.

Nevertheless, he continued, "No offense, Maddy, but I'd rather not have another social worker pounding on my door in twelve years telling me about another surprise like Rachel."

She bent down and kissed him. "It's not a problem."

"But—"

She leaned down farther, until her mouth was right beside his ear. "Trust me," she whispered. "I won't get pregnant. I guarantee it."

Then she scooted her body down the length of his until they were nearly joined together. She curled her fingers around him and guided him forward, slipping him inside her welcoming warmth before he could say another word. Carver groaned and cupped his hands over her fanny, pulling her down to push himself deeper still. After that, he couldn't have asked her another question if he'd wanted to. Then, again, words weren't exactly necessary. Because what Maddy made him feel was indescribable.

When he couldn't quite reach the depths of her he wanted to plunder, Carver rolled their bodies until their positions were switched. She gasped at the change, then tangled her legs with his, cupping her hands over his buttocks to silently urge him closer still. He buried his face in her neck and kissed her shoulder, then heaved himself forward to journey as far as he could.

And then something else—something he wasn't quite able to identify—took over. Carver was rocked by emotions and sensations he'd never experienced before. Maddy made him feel such things...wild things, crazy things, wonderful things....

He paced himself along with the crescendo of new emotions, then cried out in ecstasy and anguish at their culmination. He rolled his body again, carrying Maddy with him, and for long moments could only lie beneath her, clutching her to himself, gasping for breath, and trying to make sense of what had just happened.

"Is it over?" he finally asked. "Can I talk now?"

Her voice came to him softly, somewhere around the vicinity of his neck and shoulder. "If you're able."

He smiled. "Barely."

He thought he felt her nod against him. "Then it's okay to talk now."

"Maddy, I think..."

Too late, he realized he wasn't yet certain what exactly he wanted to tell her. What he was feeling was too new, too strange, for him to try to fully comprehend it. And anything of substance he had to say right now would necessarily be a result of those feelings. So instead of telling Maddy something she might misunderstand, something he might regret later, he threaded his fingers through her hair and pulled her head up gently until he could look into her eyes.

"Maddy, I think for an encore, we should move into the bedroom."

She smiled, looking relieved for some reason. Only then did he realize that she was as confused and unwilling to consider what was happening between them right now as he.

She shivered a little and pressed her body closer to his. "And I think we should turn on the heat, too. It's freezing in here."

Carver pushed himself up off the floor and bent to retrieve Maddy. As he carried her toward his bedroom, he cupped his hand intimately over her fanny and gave her an affectionate squeeze.

"Oh, I'll turn up the heat," he promised as he passed through his bedroom door and kicked it shut behind them with his foot. "Brace yourself, sweetheart," he added as he tossed her playfully to the middle of his bed. "'Cause we're heading for a tropical paradise."

Maddy laughed and threw her arms open wide to receive him. "Good. Because I'm long overdue for a vacation."

Eight

Carver awoke to the sound of his front door being slammed shut. Immediately, he rolled toward the other side of his bed, fearful that Maddy had run out on him before he had the chance to tell her so many of the things he wanted to reveal. But she slept peacefully beside him on her stomach, her head turned toward his, one hand loosely clutching his pillow. He smiled. Her ivory skin was touched with pink in places, and her dark hair was wonderfully mussed, both conditions a result of their physical exploits of the night before. Her bare back rising and falling with the respiration of deep slumber told him she was nowhere near waking.

Carver wanted to wake her. He even went so far as to reach out to her, ready to trace the delicate line of her spine to where the sheet and blanket dipped dangerously low over her heart-shaped fanny. Then he remembered the jarring thunder of his front door moments ago. If he and Maddy were in the bedroom, he reasoned, only one other person could have generated the noise without being guilty of breaking and entering.

Quickly, he scrambled out of bed and rifled through his dresser for a pair of jeans and a denim work shirt. He stumbled barefoot out of his bedroom, hastily buttoning himself up, and recalled too late that his and Maddy's clothes of the night before were strewn all over the living room floor. There was no way Rachel could have missed them when she'd come in.

He decided to deal with her reaction to that later. There was something a lot more pressing the two of them had to deal with now. Like where the hell Rachel had been the night before. Like the fact that he had envisioned the most gruesome scenarios about her fate. Like the fact that he had been worried sick about her....

Like the fact that he had honestly begun to wonder what would become of him without her.

Without further hesitation, Carver crossed the hallway to his daughter's bedroom and rapped loudly.

"What?" her voice sounded from the other side.

Only then was he able to expel the breath he'd been unaware of holding. Rachel sounded angry, perturbed and generally annoyed. In other words, she sounded like she always did. His daughter was okay. Safe and sound and none the worse for wear. The realization hit Carver like a Mack truck. He was relieved, happy and satisfied. And then he got really, really mad.

He tried to keep his voice calm and level as he demanded, "Rachel, open this door."

"I'm busy," she told him.

"Open the door."

"I'm busy."

He took a deep breath and tried again. "Dammit, Rachel, open the door."

"No."

There was no lock on her bedroom door, but Carver made it a point to give her the privacy any human being deserved. He would not storm in there and behave like an overwrought father, he promised himself. Even if that was exactly what he was.

"I'll say this one more time," he told her through gritted teeth, "and if you don't do as I ask, I'm coming in. Open...this...door. Now."

A door opened at that, but it wasn't Rachel's—it was Carver's. Maddy stood framed by the doorway wearing nothing but one of his plaid flannel shirts, fastening the last of the buttons. She ran a hand frantically through her hair, but to no avail. The short strands still shot up all over her head as if...well, as if they'd been ruffled by a very fervent lover.

"She's home?" Maddy asked, clearly anxious about the potential repercussions of the situation.

Carver nodded. "She's home. But she won't come out of her room."

Maddy edged past him toward the living room. "Well, let me get my clothes before you try again."

At that, Rachel's bedroom door flew open, and the girl peered out at the two adults. "Oh, gee, did I interrupt something?" she asked, her voice dripping with sarcasm.

Carver dropped his hands to his waist and glared back at her. "No, actually, we were finished. Now, where the hell have you been all night?"

Rachel seemed nonplussed by his reaction, and he took advantage of her discomposure. "Answer me," he bit out. "Maddy and I have been worried sick about you."

"Oh, yeah, I can see just how you two spent the night all wrapped up in what was happening to me."

"Don't dodge the subject," Carver told her. "Maddy and I aren't answerable to you. But you, dammit, are answerable to us."

"Carver, watch your language," Maddy said softly from behind him. "She's only a child."

He spun around to find that she had gathered up her clothes and clutched them close to her body. Her glasses sat firmly on the bridge of her nose, and she almost, almost, looked like herself again. He couldn't help but linger his gaze on her long legs extending from the hem of his shirt, though. Man, his clothes had never looked that good on him.

Then his mind reeled back to the subject of his daughter again, and he wondered if there would ever be a time when he could jibe his life with Rachel's. He fastened his gaze to hers.

Rachel's eyes were huge and accusing, and far too cognizant of what had happened between him and Maddy the night before. Not only that, he realized, but she had spent the night on the mean streets of Philadelphia and lived to tell the tale. She was too grown up for her own good, he thought. Only the spattering of freckles on her cheeks and nose reminded him that she was just a kid.

Some of his anger evaporated, and he slumped forward a little, as if succumbing to a great weight. He wondered if there was any way he could help her recapture the youth she had been robbed of by her mother's irresponsible behavior and her family's general neglect. Too late, he realized he hadn't exactly gone out of his way to help her out in that respect. Because he hadn't known the first thing about kids, he, too, had been treating Rachel as if she were an adult, forgetting that someone twenty-six years his junior needed considerably more structure in her life.

And now that he was the one responsible for her, he reminded himself further, his own life was going to require a little reorganization, too.

"I'm sorry," he said, apologizing for his lapse into adult language when he was in fact addressing a child.

"Hey, it's nothing I haven't heard before," Rachel told him, her voice snapping as tight as a whip. "Hell, it's nothing I haven't used before."

"That doesn't make it acceptable," he assured her. "For either one of us. Now, come out of your room. We have to talk."

He heard Maddy shift behind him. "I, uh ... I'll just go get dressed."

Carver nodded. "Fine. Rachel?" He extended his hand toward the living room.

She narrowed her eyes at him and opened her mouth to protest. But something in his own eyes must have made her think twice about challenging him, because she clamped her lips tight again and preceded him down the hallway.

"Sit," he instructed when they reached the living room.

Miraculously, she obeyed him, perching herself on the edge of the sofa and staring straight ahead. Carver paced the length of the room to snatch a pack of cigarettes from a bookcase, then shook one free and lit it.

"Now then," he began as he expelled a long stream of white smoke from his lungs. "Where were you last night?"

Rachel shifted a little nervously and studied the back of her hand. "I was out of smokes, so I went out for some more. While I was out, I decided to see a little more of the city."

Carver inhaled deeply on the cigarette again, not so much because he wanted to feel the heat of nicotine warming him, but because he didn't trust himself not to use profanity—lots of profanity—when he replied to Rachel's explanation for her absence.

"You went out for a pack of smokes," he finally repeated quietly, proud of himself for the level timbre of his voice.

She nodded. "Yeah."

"I see. And you decided to go sight-seeing, too."

She nodded once more.

"How nice." Carver resumed his pacing, crossing the room in four large strides before turning to complete the action again. "And did you see all the pertinent sights?" he asked. "The Liberty Bell and Constitution Hall and Penn's Landing?"

Rachel studied the back of her other hand. "No, I guess I missed those."

Carver stopped pacing in front of her and waited until she looked up at him before continuing. "Then where did you go?" he asked when she finally met his gaze. "Where have you been for the last sixteen hours?"

He wasn't sure, but he thought Rachel tossed her head defiantly before she told him, "There was a rave going on at a coffee shop up the street."

"A rave?"

"Yeah."

He wasn't sure he wanted to know the answer, but asked anyway, "What the...what on earth is a rave?"

His daughter shook her head at him as if he were the most hopeless idiot on the planet. "It's like...poetry."

Now he was really confused. "Poetry."

"Yeah, poetry. God, don't you know anything about anything?"

Carver was fast approaching the end of his rope, an end that was quickly unraveling. "I know lots of things, Rachel. I especially know when some insolent kid is trying to snow me."

"I'm not trying to snow you," she denied. "There was a rave going on at a coffeehouse up the street. I like poetry, so I went inside. It was really good, and the people were really nice, and time just got away from me, all right?"

Her expression had changed dramatically as she spoke, and if Carver hadn't known better, he might have actually been convinced that her feelings had been hurt by his mistrust. He was about to launch into another attack on her credibility when Maddy spoke softly from behind him.

"She's telling you the truth, Carver."

He spun around and found her dressed in her regular clothes, her hair now damp and fingered back into place.

"There was a rave at that coffee shop up the street last night," she told him. "I noticed it when you parked your car."

Carver's gaze ricocheted from Maddy to Rachel and back again. "You actually know what she's talking about?"

Maddy nodded. "Raves are these all-night sessions some of the coffeehouses put on. Kids dance, read poetry, sing, perform quick plays, whatever. And they drink lots of soda and coffee, so they can go on all night. Granted, the kids are usually in high school or college, but..." She looked past him to offer his daughter a brief smile. "Every now and then you find a few younger ones who fit in fine. If Rachel says that's where she was, I believe her."

Carver turned back to study his daughter in silence. "What kind of poetry?" he finally asked, still not convinced she was being completely honest about her whereabouts.

She shrugged a little nervously. "Like, I don't know. All kinds. Like Beat stuff, mostly."

His eyebrows shot up in surprise. "Beat stuff? You like Beat poetry?"

Her shoulders scrunched up again. "Well, yeah."

"Like what?" he challenged. "Give me some specifics."

"Like Ginsberg's 'America,'" she said. "Or Ferlinghetti's 'Underwear.' I like the funny ones best."

Carver chuckled a little nervously and looked at Maddy again. She smiled back and shrugged herself.

"This is too weird," he said. "I can't believe a twelve-year-old girl is reading Ginsberg and Ferlinghetti."

"Well, Mom sort of pointed me in that direction," Rachel told him. "She gave me *On the Road* for my twelfth birthday. She thought it was, you know, important."

Carver dropped his head into his hands and felt the weight of fatherhood try to squash him. Oh, boy. This parenting stuff was going to be a lot more complicated than he'd thought.

Clearly, Rachel wasn't a little girl. Twelve years old nowadays was obviously a lot older than it had been when Carver had been that age himself. Nevertheless, she was still far too young to be left to her own devices. Things could not go on between him and his daughter the way they had been. Both of them were going to have to make some changes if he ever hoped to restore some degree of sanity to their lives.

"Okay, I'll agree that you're not a typical twelve-year-old," he conceded softly as he took a seat beside Rachel on the sofa. "You're smarter, savvier and a bit more sophisticated than most kids your age."

"Like I've been telling you all along," she said, "I can take care of myself."

"And that's where I'm going to have to disagree with you," he countered.

"Hey, last night, I was smart enough to—"

"Last night, you were lucky nothing happened to you. Lucky, Rachel. Not smart."

She opened her mouth to object, but Carver continued before she could say a word.

"No matter what your life was like in L.A., no matter how much you were forced to take care of yourself because your mother was unwilling or unable to do it herself..." He sighed, started to reach out toward her, then thought better of the action. "You're still just a kid, Rachel. You're twelve years old. You ought to start acting like it. Stop trying to be an adult. Trust me. It ain't that great a gig. Enjoy your childhood while you can. Because you don't have much of it left."

He stood, dropped his hands to his hips, and met Rachel's gaze eye to eye. "Okay, here's what we're going to do," he said. "We're going to start all over again, and pretend that this is the beginning. And from now on, Rachel, you're going to have to follow some rules around here, no questions asked. There will be no more smoking, no more dressing like a bum, no more coffee, no more swearing."

"Whoa, hang on. I'm not going to—"

"You will restrict your television viewing time to one hour a day," he continued, ignoring her protest, "you will do your fair share of chores around the apartment, you will be in bed by ten o'clock every night, and you will read at least one *age appropriate* classic novel a month. *Black Beauty* might be a good start. I remember my sisters always liked that one."

"Oh, now just wait one—"

"You will, in short, behave like a human being. Because you *are* a human being, Rachel," he added meaningfully. "You're bright, funny, interesting and decent. You're a good kid, and you play an important role in the scheme of things. And..." He sighed once, hoping she wouldn't think he sounded like a sentimental jerk when he added, "And you've become very important to me."

She had dropped her head to stare into her lap when he'd reminded her that she was a human being, and she continued to avoid his gaze when he finished with his assessment of her character and her importance in his life. He sighed again, wishing he knew how to reach her.

When she continued to simply sit in silence, Carver threw his hands out to his sides and said, "Now then, those are my rules for you, and I don't want to hear any objections. There will be no objections. Got it?"

Finally, Rachel looked up, folding her arms over her chest before glaring at him, silently daring him just to try and enforce his edicts. But there was something a little less menacing about her posture than there usually was when she was about to challenge him, he thought. Her mouth wasn't set quite so tightly, and her eyes didn't glitter nearly as angrily as they usually did. Carver took it to be a good sign. Maybe she'd loosen up even more when she heard the rest of his spiel.

"In turn," he continued after a telling pause, "*I* will stop smoking and swearing and dressing like a bum, and I'll quit after two cups of coffee in the morning. I'll restrict my television viewing time to one hour a day, will do my fair share of chores around the apartment, will be in bed by midnight and will read at least one classic novel a month."

He smiled at Rachel's expression, now one of utter and irretrievable confusion.

"In short," he concluded, "I, too, will behave like a human being. No objections."

Silence greeted his offer for the first several minutes after he announced it. Rachel stood, looked first at him, then past him at Maddy, then down at the floor. She shifted her weight from one foot to the other, scratched the back of her head, inhaled a deep breath as if ready to speak at length, then exhaled again without saying a word. Finally, she looked up at Carver.

"You might, uh... You might want to start with *On the Road,*" she told him. "It's really good."

Carver grinned at her. "I know. I read it when I was twelve."

Rachel grinned back, and he was shocked and dismayed to realize it was the first smile he'd seen from the girl since she'd come to live with him. Hesitantly, not certain what kind of a reception he'd receive, he took a few steps forward and opened his arms.

"Don't panic," he told her when he saw her eyes widen in alarm. "I won't do it if you don't want me to. But I am your father," he reminded her. "It's about time I started acting like it. So... What do you say? Will you give your old man a hug?"

Maddy stood behind the pair holding her breath. She wanted to warn Carver not to rush things with Rachel, and hoped he wouldn't be hurt when his daughter shunned his overture. Then, to her amazement, Rachel took a slow, uncertain step toward him. Then another. Then another. As if neither father nor daughter were exactly sure what encompassed a loving embrace, they stumbled into a quick hug and then sprang apart again.

"Okay," Carver said when it was over. "That was good. That was a start. We just need to practice a little, but I think we'll get it down pretty well before long."

Rachel chuckled a little and ducked her head. "Yeah. Okay. Whatever." A few more uneasy moments passed before she looked up at Carver and Maddy again. When she did, it was to ask, "Uh, do you mind if I turn in? I didn't get much sleep last night."

Maddy was about to say something like, *You're not the only one,* but stopped herself when she realized how easily the statement could be misconstrued. The reason for her and Carver's sleep loss hadn't been anywhere nearly as civilized as Rachel's. Instead of listening to poetry, they'd been creating it, she thought with a fond smile. Then, upon realizing just how hokey that sounded, she knew she should go home and try to get a little shut-eye, too. Thank goodness it was Saturday.

"Go ahead," Carver told his daughter with a smile. "Sleep all day if you want. But remember, when you wake up, I have a few things for you to do around here."

"Yeah, yeah, yeah," she said as she passed him. But she, too, smiled as she did so, and Maddy got the distinct impression that Rachel wasn't nearly as unhappy about her new obligations as she was letting on.

"I have to go, too," Maddy said after Rachel had closed her bedroom door.

She moved hastily toward the front door and reached for her coat, but Carver's fingers circling her wrist stayed the action.

"Not so fast," he said.

She tried to tell herself the racing of her pulse was a simple result of the emotional scene she had just witnessed between Carver and his daughter. Unfortunately, although she could concede that Carver's actions were responsible, his daughter had nothing to do with Maddy's tumultuous feelings.

"What?" she asked, hoping her voice revealed none of the wild sensations stampeding through her.

His fingers tightened around her wrist, but Carver never said a word. Instead, he tugged gently until he brought her hand to his lips, then opened her curled fingers until he could place a soft kiss on her palm. His eyelids fluttered downward as he lowered his head to perform the gesture, as if he were bowing to the most reverent of acts. The warmth of his hands, her memory of the way he had touched her the night before, her knowledge of the physical power he possessed, all threatened to overwhelm her. Carver's hands were the kind that could easily snap her in two, but they belonged to a man who was nothing but gentle.

The realization that he was at once so strong and so tender made Maddy wish she was a girl of seventeen again. Before she had seen what the world was really like. Before she had come to realize what human beings were capable of doing to each other. Before she had been able to understand how things between a man and a woman could go so utterly awry. Before she had completely lost hope.

Slowly, carefully, she twisted her wrist until she had freed it from Carver's gentle imprisonment. She circled it with her own fingers, softly rubbing away the sensation of his warm flesh caressing hers.

"I have to go," she repeated softly.

He continued to hold his hand out toward her as if she hadn't pulled away from him, his expression one of hurt bewilderment. She wished she knew how she could make him understand that what had happened between them last night, although quite wonderful, would never happen again.

When he said nothing in response to her intention to leave, but only gazed at her as if he couldn't believe what she was doing, Maddy reached for her coat again and shrugged into it.

"I have a full day ahead of me," she tried lamely to explain.

"It's Saturday," he argued. "It's your day off."

"I have a backlog of stuff to get through like you couldn't imagine. This is the perfect day to catch up."

He glared at her then, and dropped his hands to his hips. It was the same posture he had assumed with Rachel only moments ago, suggesting that he thought Maddy was a recalcitrant child who wouldn't behave the way she was supposed to. And regardless of the fact that that was precisely what she felt like, she prepared to defend herself heartily.

"You know, Maddy," he began, his tone of voice not unlike the one he had used with Rachel earlier, either, "a lot of people who had just spent the night making wild jungle love together for the first time might look at the prospect of a free Saturday a little differently. Instead of viewing it as an opportunity to work an extra ten or twelve hours after putting in a sixty-hour week already, they might see it as a time to...oh, say...spend a little time together trying to understand the repercussions of their actions. Getting to know each other even more intimately. Even," he added, lowering his voice, "making wild jungle love again."

The glimmer in his eyes—those pale blue eyes that had haunted her for more than half a lifetime—was nearly Maddy's undoing. He was looking at her as if she were the fulfillment of a wish uttered long ago, the completion of a promise he'd never thought he would realize. He was looking at her as if he cared deeply for her. And that was something she simply couldn't let him do.

"About last night," she began, deliberately turning the event into a cliché.

"What about last night?" Carver asked when she hesitated.

"It...I..." She lowered her gaze as she stammered, "I...I just want to say thanks."

"Thanks?"

The shocked disbelief in his voice made it impossible for her to look at him, so she continued to stare at the floor as she nodded. "Yeah, thanks. You were there for me last night, Carver, and I appreciate it."

"And just what's that supposed to mean?"

She shrugged, feeling more and more like a confused kid with every breath she took. "Just that, after the kind of day I had yesterday, it was nice to have someone to turn to last night. You made me feel better. You made *me* feel like a human being again, too. You..." Finally, she tilted her head back so that she could meet his gaze levelly again. "You made me feel. Period. I wasn't sure I'd ever be able to do that again after...after what happened to Kevin Conner yesterday. So, thanks. I owe you."

He eyed her thoughtfully for a moment before repeating, "You owe me."

Not certain she could trust her voice to remain level, Maddy nodded silently.

"And all last night was to you was an opportunity to keep yourself from going numb, is that it? It was just something to jump-start your cynicism?"

"Well, if you put it like that..."

"I'm putting it like that."

Even though she disagreed with him, even though the night before had meant so much more to her than that, Maddy nodded again. "Then yes. That's all it was."

"I see."

She stuck her hand beneath her glasses and rubbed her eyes hard. Without opening them, she told him, "Look, Carver, we're both adults here. We've come a long way since high school. I think we're both smart enough to understand what last night was all about, so let's just let it go at that, okay?"

"No."

Maddy dropped her hand, and her eyes snapped open. "What?"

"I said, no. I'm not willing to let it go at that."

"Why not?"

"Because I'm not sure I *am* smart enough to understand what last night was all about. Spell it out for me, Maddy. Just what exactly happened between us last night? Aside from the fact that we shared some truly phenomenal exchanges of the physical, emotional, spiritual and carnal variety."

"Nothing happened," she snapped, trying to squash the erotic memories exploding in her brain. "We were both overwrought about something. With you, it was Rachel's disappearance, with me it was the death of a child I should have been responsible for. We turned to each other sexually in an effort to forget about our worries for a little while. That's all."

Carver chuckled, a sound devoid of any humor. "Oh, Maddy, come on. You know as well as I do that there was a hell of a lot more to it than that. This is something that's been building for twenty years, and last night, it blew up in our faces. The fallout alone is going to dog us for the next fifty years, so don't tell me you can just leave this morning without another thought for me, because I don't believe it."

He lifted his bent knuckles and rubbed them softly over her cheek. A spark of something heavy and white-hot exploded deep inside her, spiraling outward until every nerve in her body was on fire. She felt the heat creep up her throat and into her face, and she was certain Carver would know as well as she what a liar she was.

Sure enough, he whispered, "And you don't believe it, either."

She tried to feign nonchalance as she said, "You're kidding yourself, Carver. As usual, your ego is overshadowing the rest of you. Hey, I admit that last night, the sex was great. Better than I've had in a long time," she threw in for good measure. "But that's all it was. Sex."

He shook his head at her, biting his lip as if trying not to laugh at her. "Liar," he said.

She reached for the doorknob and turned it. "Look, believe whatever you want," she told him. "But I have to go."

Carver planted his palm firmly against the swiftly opening door and slammed it shut again. "You're not going anywhere until we get this settled."

"There's nothing to settle."

"Oh, yes. There is."

The absolute certainty in his voice made Maddy's head spin. When she saw the determined set of his chin and the intense look in his eyes, she knew she should have bolted when she had the chance. Before she realized what was happening, he curved one hand around her nape, and roped his arm around her waist. Then he jerked her forward against him, and plundered her mouth with his.

It was an extraordinary kiss. Quite unlike the ones he had bestowed upon her the night before. This kiss was desperate, anxious, fearful. Carver kissed her the way a man kisses a woman he knows he's going to lose, a man who will do anything to keep her from leaving. He shoved his body up against hers, pressing her hard against the front door, and held her face firmly in both hands. She felt his fingers wind fiercely through her hair, and gasped when he thrust his tongue into her mouth as if he couldn't taste her deeply enough. She felt the heart of him ripen against her belly, and she began to grow faint with wanting him.

Over and over he kissed her, plunging deeper each time, even when she thought he would split her in two if he tried to go any further. He dropped one hand to her breast and stroked the peak lovingly, a surprisingly gentle caress in light of his ferocious embrace. And all the while, he crowded his body more urgently against hers, pressing her back against the door as if he intended to send her right through it. Maddy felt every muscle, every inch of sinew marking her, as if Carver wanted to make sure he left his indelible imprint upon her forever.

And then, as quickly as he had been upon her, he pushed himself away. The two of them could only stare at each other then, amazed, appalled and completely out of breath.

"See?" Maddy finally managed to gasp out. "Sex. That's all it was. That's all it would ever be between you and me."

Carver shook his head slowly. "No," he murmured. "I've had sex before, Maddy. And it was never like what I have with you."

She fumbled behind herself for the doorknob, gripping it fiercely when she finally located it. "You did a good job with Rachel this morning," she told him on a rush of words. "You don't need me anymore."

Before he could say or do anything else that would make her crazier than she already felt, Maddy yanked open the door and fled through it. If she hadn't believed any of the other things she had said to Carver that morning, she had at least honestly meant her final words.

He was indeed doing a good job with his daughter. And he would never have need of Maddy again. Carver didn't realize what he was getting himself into with her, but she did. And it was up to her to make sure that things between them didn't go any further than they already had.

Carver didn't need her. And she didn't need Carver. As long as she kept telling herself that, things would be all right.

She only wished she could convince herself that that was true.

Nine

Maddy was staring at her hot corned beef on rye, French fries and clam chowder, wondering what on earth had possessed her to order such a big lunch in the first place, when something made her look up. The deli across the street from her office was crowded—not surprising seeing as how it was just past noon—and she scanned the faces quickly, not quite certain what she was looking for. When no one looked back, she shrugged and returned her attention to the food heaped on her plate.

She had been hungry when she ordered, she recalled vaguely. But then, she had been thinking about Carver when she ordered, too. Now that her lunch had arrived, it was curiously unappetizing. She shoved her plate away, folded her arms over each other on the table, rested her head upon them, and sighed deeply.

Two mornings ago, she had told Carver he didn't need her. Two mornings ago, she had thought she could live with that. Unfortunately, forty-eight hours of missing him had only reassured her of just what a fool she had become. Because before she had made love with Carver, Maddy had only had some vague idea of how it would be between the two of them. Now she knew. And now, she was doomed to replay that single night over and over in her brain for the rest of her life. Because no matter how badly she wanted to, there was no way she could ever allow herself to relive it.

"Maddy."

His voice came to her as it had that night, soft and lusty and full of affection. When she looked up, she saw Carver standing on the other side of her table, his cheeks burnished from the cold, his hair cascading over his forehead, no doubt a casualty of the blustery autumn wind. His leather bomber jacket hung open over a Columbia University sweatshirt and well-worn jeans, and he appeared to have neglected his morning toilette. A rough stubble of beard shadowed the lower half of his face like a dark glove, and his eyes were smudged below by faint purple crescents. He looked about as good as she felt, she thought. Nevertheless, it would be so nice to embrace him.

"What are you doing here?" she asked him.

"I'm following you."

Her eyebrows shot up in surprise. "You're what?"

"I followed you here."

She eyed him curiously for a moment before saying, "I spurned you the other night, and now you're stalking me for it, is that it?"

He shoved two big hands restlessly through his hair, then pulled out the empty chair on the other side of the table and slumped into it. "Although I've gone without enough sleep the past three nights that I'm almost crazy enough to understand the guys who do stuff like that, no. I'm not stalking you. I was coming to see you at your office, and as I drove by the building, I saw you leave and come here. It's taken me a while to find a parking space."

"Oh."

"Oh?" he echoed. "That's all you can say?"

She pulled her plate toward her again, more because she needed something to occupy her hands than because she wanted the food. "What am I supposed to say?"

"I don't know. But one single syllable that's really more a sound than a word seems somehow inadequate for everything we need to say to each other."

She picked up a French fry and toyed with it for a moment. "Okay then. How about if I just ask you again. What are you doing here?"

"I needed to see you."

She dropped the limp piece of potato back onto her plate and avoided Carver's eyes. "About what? I told you you're doing a good job with Rachel and I meant it. That deal you struck with her was perfect. It was just what she needed. Some rules and guidelines, but also a signal that you're willing to make some changes in your life along with hers. You're going to be a good father, Carver. You don't need me there anymore."

"That's where you're wrong, Maddy." He reached his hand across the table to take hers, so she quickly withdrew her own and tucked them into the pockets of her brown tweed blazer. He tipped his forehead to acknowledge her retreat, then threaded his own fingers together before him.

He took a deep breath and expelled it slowly before continuing. "I don't deny that things between me and Rachel are starting to look up. You had a lot to do with that—with making me see how things were with her. And with making me see how things were with me. I've done a lot of soul-searching the past couple of days. The more I look at how I was living before you and Rachel came into my life, and at the changes the two of you have brought with you, the more I see how much I've been missing."

A waitress approached them then, and asked Carver if he'd like to order. He mumbled a few words to which Maddy didn't pay attention, because she was too busy trying to ward off what she could feel coming next. Somehow, she was certain that Carver was going to tell her things she didn't want to hear. But for the life of her, she couldn't think of a single way to stop him.

When the waitress left, he started talking again. "Because of a daughter I never knew I had, I'm developing this newly settled lifestyle that seems as if it's going to be oddly enjoyable. It's going to be more predictable, more stable, more...more normal. I've made some concessions in my life where Rachel is concerned, concessions I never thought I'd make, but ones that are actually improving the way I live. What's really strange is that I'm willing—I'm actually eager—to make more."

Maddy didn't know what made her ask the question, but she couldn't stop herself from saying, "Like what?"

He hesitated for a moment before replying. "Well, like...like I think it would be nice if my life included a meaningful, and hopefully lasting, relationship with a woman. What do you think?"

She, too, paused before answering him, to gather her wits about her and to choose her words very carefully. "I think...I think that would be good," she heard herself say, proud of herself for keeping her voice completely free of emotion. "For...for you and Rachel both. You need a stable influence as much as she does."

He nodded slowly and eyed her intently. "I'm glad to hear you say that. Because there's one woman in particular that I have in mind for the job. If she'll have me."

The warning bells Maddy had been waiting for went off in her brain with the quickness and menace of a house afire. She didn't want to hear anything more he had to say, didn't want to know the particulars of what was going on in that wily, misguided brain of his. Whatever plan Carver had in mind, if it included the two of them, it would never work. There were a number of reasons for that, all of them good, she thought, but she was certain he wouldn't accept any of them. Therefore, her only recourse was to stop him now, before he said something they were both going to regret.

"I have to get back to work," she blurted out, shoving her chair away from the table with enough force to send it toppling backward. "I didn't realize how late it is."

Carver looked puzzled. "It's not late, Maddy. You were just getting started with your lunch."

"It's late," she repeated as she searched through her purse for her wallet. "Trust me. It's late."

"Sit down," he instructed her calmly. "You're not going anywhere until I've finished with what I have to tell you."

Maddy supposed it was inevitable that she and Carver would have to eventually confront whatever strange fire had risen up between them. It was too intense, too undying and had been burning for too long. It wasn't likely to be extinguished just because she wanted it to. So, slowly, she closed her purse, righted her chair, and sat precariously on the edge of it. Then she folded her hands primly before her, looked him right in the eye and said, "Okay, say whatever it is you want to say. Then I have to get back to work."

Her encouragement seemed to act as a signal for him to withdraw, because for a long moment, Carver never said a word. He only studied her as if she were some fascinating biological specimen under glass that he was trying to figure out. *Socialworkerus changetheworldus,* she thought whimsically. A species near the brink of extinction. Maybe Carver was trying to figure out how to bring the whole breed back in numbers. Too bad he didn't realize contemporary society simply couldn't accommodate such a life form. Contemporary society was what had killed it off in the first place.

"You were saying..." she said quietly in an effort to make him get on with it. The sooner she could escape, the better.

Carver blinked, feeling for a moment as if he had forgotten where he was or what he was going to say. Then he remembered Friday night. He remembered all the things he had felt while he and Maddy were making love. He recalled their misspent youth and the strange mixture of emotions he had experienced at eighteen, recalled all the things he could have told Maddy then, had he even vaguely understood his adolescent confusion. He remembered all the things he wanted to say to her now. So he rested his elbows on the table and leaned forward, deliberately crowding himself into her space.

"I was saying that I'm actually beginning to enjoy all the changes in my life that Rachel has brought with her. And that I'm actually looking forward to the ones yet to come."

Maddy almost smiled at him. Her lips did in fact complete the gesture, but the look in her eyes countered any levity that her mouth conveyed. The realization didn't sit well with him at all.

"That's good, Carver," she said, her voice no happier than her expression. "I'm very happy for you."

"I was hoping to hear that you would be happy for us."

She shrugged. "Okay. I'm happy for you and Rachel both."

Carver shook his head. "No, I didn't mean 'us' as in me and Rachel. I meant 'us' as in me and you."

This time Maddy was the one to blink as if she had forgotten where she was. "Oh."

He frowned. "There's that sound again."

"What sound?"

"That *oh* sound you seem to be so good at. And I don't like hearing it this time any more than I did the first time. Just what does 'Oh' mean, anyway?"

She sighed, tucking the fingers of both hands beneath her glasses to rub her eyes. She seemed to do that a lot, Carver thought, rubbing her eyes when he was around. And for some reason, he got the feeling she didn't do it so much because her eyes were bothering her as she did because she didn't want to look at him.

"Normally, in conversation, I suppose it's an expression of resolution," she said softly.

"Resolution," he repeated. "I see. And just what exactly have we resolved here?"

She dropped her hands and gazed at him levelly. "We've resolved that *you* want something from our relationship that doesn't coincide with what *I* want."

"Is that a fact?"

"Yes, it's a fact."

"So you're a mind reader now, is that it?"

"No, of course not."

"Then how do you know what I want?"

"Okay, I don't know what you want," she amended. "But I do know what you *think* you want."

He chuckled dryly. "Well, that's good. It's nice that one of us knows so well what I want. I only hope you know what you want, too, because I sure as hell don't."

Her lips thinned into a tight line. "Then allow me to explain things to you the way I see them."

"Please, by all means explain my own hopes and desires for me. Evidently you have no faith in the fact that I might be able to understand them myself."

"Fine. I will," she snapped. She, too, leaned forward over the table, bringing her face to within inches of his. "Less than a month ago," she began, clearly straining to be civil, "you were hit right between the eyes with a daughter you never knew you had. Literally overnight, you became a father with a fully grown kid you didn't have a clue about raising. You needed some guidance. You got it from an old friend—me."

"Come on, Maddy, you know we're so much more than old friends...."

She ignored him and continued. "Now things between you and Rachel are looking up. It appears that the two of you are eventually going to work through this just fine. As a result, you're overcome by these rosy feelings of wanting a normal, happy family life, one complete with wife and mother. And because I happen to remind you of a simpler time in your life, because I'm the most recent romantic entanglement you've had, because of some lusty youthful attraction we satisfied the other night—"

"Satisfied, Maddy? Speak for yourself. I'd say that night only inflamed the attraction to the melting point."

"Because of all those things," she continued without acknowledging him, "you think I might be a likely candidate for the job. Am I pretty much on track here?"

"Pretty much," he conceded. "Although I think the reasons you listed are a bit shy of the truth. The reason I think you might be a likely candidate has nothing to do with our past history or your sudden reappearance into my life. The reason for it is because I'm beginning to realize that I have some very serious, very deep-seated feelings for you that are anything but adolescent in nature."

"Well, you're wrong about that."

Carver was about to launch into a really good how dare you assume to understand my feelings tirade when their waitress returned with his BLT and soda. He waited silently while the young woman arranged his lunch on the table before him and asked politely if there was anything else she could get him. He was about to tell her that yes, there was, that if she could bring him a glass of ice water for him to toss in Maddy's face to make her sit up and take stock of reality, he'd be much obliged. Instead, he used the time to calm himself down, told the waitress he was perfectly content with the way his lunch had turned out, at least, and that there was nothing more he needed. Nothing that she could bring him anyway.

Then he returned his attention to the woman who sat opposite him. "I'm wrong about that," he repeated blandly.

"Yes."

"Wrong about my own emotions."

"Yes."

"Wrong about the fact that I think I've fallen in love with you."

She did have the decency to blush when he told her that. He supposed he should take some stock in the fact that she showed some kind of response, even if she didn't say a word to acknowledge she had even heard him.

"Wrong about the fact that I think I've fallen hopelessly, irrevocably in love with you," he clarified. "The kind of love that lasts through two decades of separation, long past a teenaged infatuation that in itself was pretty intense. The kind of love that explodes into a frenzy of physical demand like the one the two of us enjoyed the other night. The kind of love a man feels for a woman when he's certain he can't live without her. Wrong about that, am I?''

The pink stain in her cheeks became red, and her gaze darted to her left. ''Yes,'' she finally said. ''You're wrong about that.''

''I see. And how, may I ask, can you be so certain that I'm so wrong?''

Maddy's gaze remained diverted for some moments, then suddenly returned to meet Carver's. Met his intensely and dead on target. ''Because there's no such thing as a love like that,'' she told him without an ounce of skepticism. ''There's no such thing as a meaningful, lasting, *loving* relationship.''

She honestly believed that, Carver realized with no small amount of astonishment. She was truly of the opinion that feelings of deep, long-lasting affection didn't exist. More than that, she was convinced of it.

In spite of his certainty, however, he said, ''You don't believe that, Maddy.''

''Yes, I do,'' she replied without hesitation.

''You can't.''

''I do.''

''But what about...what about your parents? My parents? Our folks had great relationships. And don't try to tell me otherwise, Maddy, because you know what I'm saying is true.''

She nodded. ''You're right. Our parents did have solid, loving marriages. But they grew up and died in completely different times. Marriages, relationships like that were possible in our parents' time, but not now. The world's a different place now. People are different. Relationships are different. And they just don't last anymore.''

''Look, just because your first marriage didn't work out doesn't mean—''

"It's not just me and Dennis, Carver. It's everywhere. In my job, I've seen a million families break apart. I've seen what happens to people who thought they loved each other at one time. Who thought they wanted a family. And who realized pretty quickly that the reality of Mom and Pop and kids seated around the Thanksgiving turkey doesn't look anything at all like the Norman Rockwell storybook version. Too often, that Mom is alcoholic and that Pop is abusive and those apple-cheeked kids are torturing neighborhood pets and starting fires in their spare time." She leaned in closer. "Here's a news flash for you, Carver—Life isn't the cover of the *Saturday Evening Post*."

"It's not the cover of *Psychology Today*'s dysfunctional issue, either," he shot back.

She relented at that. "You're right. Not every family is dysfunctional. But even the best ones fall apart."

"Not always," he pointed out.

"Too often," she countered.

"But not always."

She gazed at him in silence for a moment. "I've seen too many families destroyed. Why would I want to start one of my own?"

"Maybe because you'd know how to do it right."

She uttered a small sound at that, something that was at once sad and wistful and longing. But she said nothing in response to his assertion. Carver decided that maybe her silence wasn't such a bad thing. It gave him a chance to elaborate, a chance to change her mind.

"All I'm asking is that you give this thing between us a chance. You and I were starting to get along great. Friday night was incredible. We make a good couple, you and I. We'd make a good family."

More warning bells erupted in Maddy's muddled brain at Carver's roughly uttered declaration. Something about it troubled her even more than anything else he'd said so far.

"What do you mean by that?" she asked softly, not certain she wanted to hear his answer.

He smiled at her, a warm, fuzzy, toe-curling smile that was almost too much to resist. "I mean just what I said. You and I would make a good family. We're reasonably intelligent, relatively good-looking... You've got a good sense of responsibility, I've got a good sense of humor..." His smile broadened. "Let's face it, we've got good genes. You always said you wanted a passel of kids when we were kids. I always said you were nuts. But now..."

She sucked in an anxious breath. "Now...?"

He settled his chin in his hand, a posture that left him looking handsome and winsome and thoroughly at peace. "Now I'm beginning to understand the attraction," he told her.

"You... you want a bigger family?" she asked. "As in, you want to have more children?"

He nodded and smiled again. "Yeah, I think I do. It's crazy, isn't it? But I can't quite rid myself of the thought of having more kids."

"Then you're out of luck again," she told him. "Because even if I thought things between the two of us, by some wild miracle, could work out, I won't have children."

"Look, Maddy, if this is about your job, about all the suffering you see kids go through, that wouldn't be an issue with us. We'd love our children to distraction. We'd give them the best of everything."

She expelled that oddly sad laugh again. "Listen to you. Already making out Christmas lists."

"Hey, why wait until the last minute?"

"Because I just told you, Carver. I won't have children with you. I can't."

"But, Maddy—"

"Carver, I can't. Don't you understand? I *can't.*"

He looked mildly bemused, then realization seemed to dawn on him. Dawned on him like a good, solid blow to the back of his head, she thought sadly.

"What do you mean?" he asked.

"I mean thanks to a very serious bout with endometriosis when I was in college, I am physically unable to have children. If you want that Norman Rockwell turkey thing complete with kids, you'll have to look somewhere else. Because you won't be getting it from me."

He said nothing in reply to her announcement, a response Maddy took to be less than encouraging. What the hell? she thought. He might as well know it all.

"It's why Dennis and I split up," she told him. "Before we were married, he said remaining childless wouldn't be a problem, that he didn't care about having kids. But somewhere along the line, he did start to care. And because I couldn't give him a family, he decided to find someone who could."

Once again, Carver's response to her revelation was silence. He didn't seem to be upset or angry or disappointed. He simply seemed to be... confused. Maddy sympathized. She had been confused for a long time, too. Nowadays, however, everything was perfectly clear to her.

This time when she pushed her chair away from the table, it was with a slow, unnerving scrape. "It's not that I don't want children, Carver. But this is how things have turned out for me. I made my peace with my fate a long time ago, and I'm as content as I can be with the way my life is. All in all, it's not nearly as unfulfilled as some of the lives I've seen."

She stood and moved to stand beside him, but he continued to stare wordlessly at the seat she had vacated. "I can be relatively happy without the kind of life you want," she said as she settled a hand briefly on his shoulder, hoping he couldn't detect the lie she heard so strongly in her voice. "But something tells me it wouldn't be as easy for you to give up the fantasy as it has been for me. I'm sorry. But like I said, life isn't perfect. There's always something that's going to screw up an otherwise adequate relationship."

And with that, she turned and picked her way carefully toward the exit, hoping all the while that Carver wouldn't follow her, hoping at the same time that he would.

But he didn't. And maybe, Maddy thought as she pushed her way out into the cold afternoon, that was the most telling evidence of all that the two of them just didn't have what it took to make each other happy.

Ten

Maddy's departure—or rather her flight—from Carver left him to face the other woman in his life alone. For the most part, however, he had few complaints about his developing relationship with his daughter. During the month that followed Maddy's retreat, Carver found Rachel to be a surprisingly reasonable kid, someone who was eager to please and grateful to be praised. She was quick-witted and articulate once he got her talking, something that only reinforced his conviction that she was generally more advanced than what he assumed the typical twelve-year-old must be. She had a wry sense of humor and a frightening amount of savvy. He was daily amazed at how much the two of them found to talk about.

It became a morning ritual for them to share the paper, and Carver was stunned when Rachel turned out to be an even bigger news junkie than he was. At some point, she had invited herself to raid his CD and vinyl collection, and he felt a thrill of delight every time she raved about how much she liked "The Last Waltz" or "Hotel California" or "Love It to Death." In turn, Carver found himself warming to bands like Counting Crows, Spin Doctors and Deadeye Dick. He helped her with her homework. She helped him balance his checkbook. And when she decided to become more environmèntally conscientious by adopting a vegetarian diet, they discovered the joys of broccoli and bean sprouts together.

Things still weren't perfect by any means, however. Rachel continued to have occasional outbursts of misdirected adolescent outrage that Carver simply couldn't understand or abide. And he did come home from work in the middle of the day once to find her and her friend Lanette watching a rented copy of *Friday the Thirteenth Part Whatever* when he had expressly forbidden her viewing of such violence, not to mention when she should have been at school. He still balked at letting her get her nose pierced. She still complained that he was too old to relate.

Nevertheless, the skirmishes of adversity slowly diminished, and the bouts of collaboration increased. Gradually, father and daughter settled into a fairly comfortable, if not exactly quiet, routine.

There was only one thing missing, Carver thought now as he warily watched his daughter put the finishing touches on what she had christened Rachel's Rutabaga Surprise. Maddy. Maddy was missing from his life. His and Rachel's both. Because even though Rachel had never said anything about Maddy's sudden disappearance, he could sense somehow that she missed her, too.

"So, what exactly is the 'Surprise' part of this recipe?" he asked his daughter for perhaps the tenth time.

Rachel scraped the last of the purplish yellow mixture from the bowl and smoothed it into a casserole pan. Although his knowledge of rutabagas was limited, Carver was pretty sure they weren't that color. In fact, he couldn't imagine much of anything that was that color. Nothing that was edible, anyway.

"I'll tell you after you have a taste," she said as she licked a substantial glop of the concoction from the back of her hand.

He waited to see if she would suffer any ill effects as a result. When she didn't, he found some comfort, but still harbored a heavy measure of doubt. "I think I'd rather know before I have a taste."

"No, 'cause then you'd never taste it."

"That's why I want to know in advance."

"Come on, where's your sense of adventure? Quit being such a pain." She shook her head. "Man, you have been so cranky lately."

"That's because I'm trying to quit smoking. You haven't exactly been a picnic yourself, you know."

She smiled. "This is going to be good—you'll see," she told him. "Lanette's mom makes this all the time."

"Then why are you calling it *Rachel's* Rutabaga Surprise?"

"I made a few alterations."

"Uh-huh. Like what?"

"You'll see," she repeated. "Trust me."

Yeah, right, Carver thought. *The last time I put that much faith in an adolescent girl, she still had me spinning on my ear twenty years after the fact.*

"Why don't you call Maddy and invite her to dinner?"

Rachel's casually offered question snapped Carver out of his reverie like a slingshot. "What?"

She didn't look up from her task as she repeated, "Maddy. Why don't you invite her over for dinner tonight? You guys don't seem to see too much of each other lately, and I think she'd like this."

Carver wasn't sure how to explain to Rachel what had happened between him and Maddy. But not because he didn't think a twelve-year-old claimed the ability to comprehend such a breakup. And not because he was afraid Rachel's feelings might be hurt at the realization that someone she had started to care for would possibly be removed from her life for good. No, the main reason Carver didn't know how to explain his separation from Maddy was because he wasn't sure he understood it himself.

He hadn't tried to contact her since their last meeting, simply because he didn't know what to say to her. She had dropped a bomb on him a month ago, there was no question about that. He had been stunned by her declaration that she was unable to have children. Not because *he* so badly wanted kids *now,* but because *she* had wanted kids when the two of them had been teenagers. She'd wanted them badly. He couldn't imagine what it had cost her to accept the fact that she would remain childless. He'd never been denied something he'd wanted that much.

Oh, wait, yes he had, he remembered. He'd been denied Maddy.

That afternoon a month ago, she had told him she had made peace with her fate. That she was as happy and as content as she could be. But somehow, Carver didn't quite believe that. And he didn't think Maddy did, either. He just wasn't sure how to go about making her realize or accept it. No more than he knew how to convince her that her inability to have children was completely immaterial to him.

He would be lying if he said that he didn't want to have more children beyond Rachel. Since his daughter's sudden arrival in his life, Carver had wondered a lot about the growing up she'd done before, growing up that he had missed. And a little part of him still harbored a desire to father another child. He wanted to know what it would be like to witness the birth of life and watch his child inhale that first gasp of breath. Wanted to experience the thrill and pride of watching a child take her first steps and utter her first words. Wanted to share in the wonder of a baby's single-minded fascination with something as simple as a button or a piece of string. A part of Carver would always want to experience those things. And, if the truth was told, he would always miss them.

But he would miss Maddy's presence in his life more. A lot more. He could live without having another child. But he wasn't certain he was going to make it without Maddy. He just didn't know how he would ever be able to convince her of that. Her first husband had told her the same thing. And her first husband had taken a powder when he'd changed his mind. Why should Maddy believe that Carver would be any different?

"Uh, Rachel . . ." he began.

She continued with her dinner preparations as she uttered a distracted "Hmm?"

"About Maddy and me . . ."

"Yeah?"

"Uh, we could try inviting her to dinner tonight, but I don't think she'd come."

"Why not?"

"Because . . . because I don't think she wants to see me."

That was enough to make Rachel pay attention. She gazed at him with wide blue eyes that made him feel as if he were staring into a mirror. "Why not?" she repeated.

"We sort of, um, split up."

Her expression clouded, and she seemed to become agitated about something. "Because of me, right? Because I showed up on the scene."

Carver crossed the kitchen in three long strides to drape his arm over her shoulder. He still wasn't completely comfortable with physical displays of affection—and neither was Rachel, he knew—but the two of them were gradually getting better at it. He gave her shoulder a quick squeeze before pulling away again to give her some breathing space.

"No, we did not split up because of you. You're the one who brought us together."

She smiled. "Oh."

He scrubbed a hand thoughtfully over his rough jaw. "It's kind of complicated."

"Complicated how?"

He sighed, wondering where to begin. "I've known Maddy since we were teenagers."

Rachel grinned. "Since the Stone Age, huh?"

He grimaced. "Please, I'm not that old. It was the Ice Age when Maddy and I went to school together."

Rachel grinned again. "Oh. Sorry."

"No problem."

He told her about his youthful exploits with Maddy, about how the two of them had driven each other crazy throughout high school, had gone their separate ways for college and had been reunited by Rachel's arrival in Philadelphia. He told her about how he supposed he'd never stopped caring for Maddy. And he told her about the changes in Maddy that he hadn't been able to comprehend. And then suddenly, out of nowhere, he began to understand.

Back in high school, Maddy hadn't been the only one who'd thought she could change the world. Even though he'd been unwilling to admit it then, Carver had thought she could, too. He'd chosen the cynic's way for himself, had accepted that the world was a rotten place and that the only thing left to do was expose that rottenness to the light. But Maddy had taken the high road. She'd chosen to see the good and work on that instead. Maddy... Maddy had been the light.

Somewhere along the way, however, that light had dimmed. It hadn't gone out completely, but it was sputtering for life. Maddy had experienced a few rough spots, he thought. Hell, she'd been to the earth's ugly underbelly and back again. Fate had dealt her an unkindly hand in denying her something she'd always wanted—children. Then, to make matters worse, fate had given her a job to make her feel grateful for her loss by showing her how much worse others had it. No wonder Maddy had lost her optimistic bloom, he thought. Life had ripped it right off of her.

"Rachel," he said, not certain what he planned to do, but knowing he had to do something. "We've got to help Maddy out."

"Boy, I'll say. Her life sucks."

He frowned at his daughter. "I've told you how I feel about you using that language."

"That's not swearing."

"But it is offensive."

"I've heard you say it a million times."

"I'm a jaded old man. I've earned the right. I've told you over and over that you have to pay your dues if you—"

"Yeah, yeah, yeah, I know. I gotta pay my dues if I wanna sing the blues. And I know. It don't come easy. But I still don't understand what that means."

"It's incredible wisdom," he assured her. "Someday you'll thank me."

"And I don't understand what it has to do with me using offensive language, either," she added.

"We were talking about Maddy."

"Actually, *you* were talking about Maddy. And no offense, Carver, but you make me wanna hurl with all the drooling you do whenever you say her name."

He opened his mouth to deny the charge, wasn't sure he could in all honesty do so, and chose to ignore it. Instead, he said, "You and I have a job to do where Maddy's concerned. I need your help."

"Yeah? With what?"

"We've got to help Maddy get back that fiery righteous indignation that made her so driven so long ago. We have to find out what made her lose hope and help her get it back again. We have to show her that some things in life do turn out for the better. And we have to make her see that the world can change as long as it has people like her in it."

"Uh-huh. Okay. And how are we gonna make that happen?"

"I'm working on it."

Rachel nodded. "In the meantime, I'll check the ruta-bagas."

"You do that."

When the telephone rang at 10:00 p.m., Maddy was certain somehow that it must be Carver calling, even though it had been over a month since she had heard from him. For that reason, she was inclined not to answer. But when the ringing went on for more than a minute, finally totalling twenty-two, she couldn't stand it any longer. She snatched the receiver from its resting place and snapped, "Hello."

"Maddy?"

A young person's voice from the other end of the line called out to her in distress, and immediately Maddy felt guilty for neglecting the phone. Her number was unlisted. She gave it out only when absolutely necessary, and usually to kids she thought were in some kind of danger. If her phone rang this late at night, it was generally because someone was in trouble. And anyway, why would Carver be calling her? she thought further. He'd made it clear just how little he wanted to do with her now that he knew she wasn't the Fertile Crescent.

"Yes, this is Madelaine Garrett," she told her unknown caller. "Who is this?"

The voice hesitated a moment before replying very quietly, "It's Rachel. Rachel Stillman. Do you remember me?"

As if I could forget the person who brought Carver Venner back into my life, Maddy thought dryly. Then another thought struck her. Things had been going pretty well with Carver and Rachel the last time she had seen them. If Rachel was calling her now, it could only be because something had happened. Something that probably wasn't good. She inhaled a deep breath and told herself not to worry, then ran a shaky hand through her hair.

"Of course I remember you, Rachel," she said as calmly as she could. "What's wrong? Where are you?"

Rachel sounded alarmed and terrified when she replied, her words rushed together like an express train out of control. "I...I don't know where I am. I had a fight with Carver, and I ran out of the apartment and got on a bus. It left me here, but I don't know where here is. I don't have any money, and I'm afraid to go home. I didn't know who else to call. I have your card in my wallet. I don't know what to do. I'm so scared."

Great, Maddy thought. This was just great. A frightened kid stranded out in the middle of nowhere who had no one to turn to but her. Just what she needed on a Friday night after a week spent wondering whether she'd be better off performing some really world-saving work like carpet cleaning or tending bar.

"Okay, don't panic," she said, uncertain whether the instructions were meant for Rachel or for herself. "Look around. Do you see any street signs? Any landmarks? Anything that might help me figure out where you are?"

"I...I don't think I'm in Philadelphia anymore. But I don't think I'm in New Jersey or Delaware, either. The bus didn't cross any bridges. This place looks really...rural or something." She paused for a moment, and when her voice came over the phone again, Maddy could tell the girl was barely keeping her fear under control. "It's dark. And it's starting to rain. I'm at a pay phone in front of some kind of hotel or something."

A hotel, Maddy reiterated to herself. Depending on the kind of hotel, Rachel could either be in very good shape or in really serious trouble. "What's the name of the hotel?"

After a brief moment of silence, Rachel told her, "The sign says... Houseman Inn."

"Never heard of it."

"It looks like a big house."

Okay, that was helpful, Maddy thought. That narrowed it down to about a couple hundred square miles that could be either north or west of the city. "Like maybe a bed-and-breakfast kind of thing?"

"Yeah, I guess so."

"Could you maybe be in Bucks County? There are a lot of places like that up there."

"I don't know."

Maddy began to unbutton her pajamas as she prowled around her bedroom in search of her clothes. "What street are you on?"

Another short pause, then Rachel's voice came over the line again, sounding even more frightened than before. "I don't know. I don't know what street it is. I don't know where I am. Help me, Maddy. I don't know what to do."

She sounded near tears, and Maddy couldn't quite tamp down her own frustration and fear at being unable to get to the girl *now*. "Okay, Rachel, don't worry. I'll find out where the Houseman Inn is, and I'll be there in less than an hour. If the place looks like it's safe, go inside and sit in the lobby or someplace that's crowded and well lit. If anyone says anything to you, tell them you're waiting for your mother, who's gone upstairs to your room for a minute, okay?"

When Rachel didn't reply, Maddy began to grow more concerned. "Rachel? Honey? Are you still there? Are you going to be all right? Will you do what I just told you to do?"

Her voice was very small, very distant and very scared when she finally answered. "I'm still here. I'm okay. I'll do what you say. But, Maddy?"

"Yes?"

"Hurry, okay?"

"I'll be there just as soon as I can." Maddy was dressed in jeans and a baggy brown sweater before she even said goodbye.

In the lobby of the Houseman Inn in Bucks County, Rachel settled the pay phone back in its receiver and sighed with much contentment. Man, if that wasn't an Academy Award winning performance, she didn't know what was. Meryl Streep had nothing on her. Maybe she'd go back to

L.A. someday and try her hand at acting. Obviously, she was just oozing with talent.

But first, she had one more call to make.

She dug another quarter out of her pocket, slipped it into the slot and dialed her home phone number. "Carver?" she said when he picked up the receiver at the other end.

She waited for him to complete his worried father routine, listening patiently until he finished railing about where the heck was she and didn't she realize how worried he was when he came home to find her gone, et cetera, et cetera, et cetera—a routine that she was actually starting to kind of like—then continued, "I know I'm late. I'm sorry. I got on the wrong bus or something and wound up in Bucks County. I don't have enough cash to get home...."

It wasn't enough that Rachel still scared the hell out of him daily, Carver thought as he tried to squint between the runnels of water cascading down his windshield. Now she had to be doing it on a dark and stormy night, too.

Where the hell was he, anyway? he wondered as he glanced once again at the crumpled map in the passenger seat beside him. There were no lights on the road, nothing but blackness and a slapdash stream of rain that reflected his headlights right back at him in an annoying glare. And how the hell had Rachel managed to get on a bus that stranded her in Bucks County in the first place?

Carver, watch your language.

Maddy's voice came to him from the dark recesses of his brain, chastising him even in her absence. Why did that still happen? he wondered. Why couldn't she just leave him alone? He had too much on his mind right now with locating his daughter and making sure she was safe. He didn't have the time or energy to worry about Maddy, too.

His front tire hit a deep rut and the car bounced precariously close to a ditch. At least he thought it was a ditch. Who could tell in this weather?

A brief flash of red taillights stained the darkness ahead of him, reassuring Carver that he wasn't entirely alone in the world after all. Evidently, some other poor sap had been summoned out into this mess, too. He nudged the brake with his foot and took advantage of his slowed speed to glance over at the map again. He was on the right road and nearing the intersection he had circled in red. If his calculations were correct—and Carver's sense of direction was indisputably the best in the universe, he knew—then he should be coming up on the Houseman Inn right about...

Now! he realized when he looked up again to discover that a huge, rambling Victorian bed-and-breakfast had sprung up out of nowhere. He quickly spun the steering wheel to the right and skidded into the inn's parking lot on a spray of wet gravel and a string of colorful words. He somehow bounced his car into a vacant parking space, leapt out of his seat and sprinted through the rain to the hotel's entrance.

Inside the lobby, there was some kind of small ruckus going on at the registration desk, but Carver ignored it as he scanned the room for his daughter. When he didn't see Rachel anywhere, he scanned the room again, this time dissecting it detail by detail in an effort to locate her. But Rachel was nowhere to be seen. Only then did he allow his small panic to expand into a barely controlled terror. He turned to the registration desk for help and found that the small ruckus had turned into a rather large one. A woman was having words with the desk clerk, words that weren't particularly friendly. A wet woman. An attractive woman. A woman who seemed very familiar somehow.

What was Maddy doing...?

Understanding suddenly smacked Carver square between the eyes, and immediately, his panic evaporated. Something had been bothering him ever since he'd received Rachel's phone call nearly an hour ago, and only now did he realize what it was. His daughter had been living with him for nearly two months, covering the city—by bus—in an effort to familiarize herself with her new digs. She'd visited malls and museums, parks and playgrounds, school and sight-seeing attractions. She knew how the SEPTA bus system worked better than he did. There was no way she would have gotten on one that would take her to Bucks County. Not unless Bucks County was precisely where she wanted to go.

He knew then exactly what Maddy was doing here. Like him, she had been suckered into driving through a god-awful night to visit this place, this...this... Carver sighed and took in his surroundings again, noting them a bit differently now that he wasn't terrified for the life of his daughter.

The Houseman Inn was a pretty nice place, he thought with a satisfied nod. Lace curtains, soft lighting, muted colors, Victorian furniture. The owners had done the lobby up right for the holidays, with sprays of fresh holly and evergreen decorating the mantel and banisters. Huge wreaths hung above the fireplace and registration desk, and a massive tree spattered with gold tinsel and ornaments sparkled in candlelight in the corner of the room.

The bedrooms were probably similarly decorated, he thought further, and probably came complete with fireplaces, potted plants and fresh flowers. The housekeepers probably left little chocolates on the pillows at night, and soaps shaped like butterflies on the bathroom sink. Rachel had scoped the place out nicely. The Houseman Inn was a quaint, tranquil little bed-and-breakfast with all the trappings of a romantic rendezvous.

He sauntered slowly toward the registration desk and wondered how Maddy was going to react when she found out what Rachel had done to them.

She was still railing at the desk clerk when Carver approached her, roaring something about how could the man leave an unattended child...well, unattended? He let her go on for a few minutes more before he cut in.

"This guy probably left the child unattended," he told Maddy, "because the child in question is more of a con artist than a kid."

Maddy spun around to face him so quickly that Carver extended an arm to keep her from revolving right out the door. He pulled her into his arms, held her tight, and smiled at the expression on her face—one of shock, censure and surprise. And more than anything else in the world, he wanted to kiss her. Kiss her so hard that neither one of them was sure if the sun would ever rise again.

"Hi," he said quietly.

"Hi," she replied automatically, still obviously quite confused.

"It's nice to see you again."

"It's nice to see you, too."

"So, what do you say? You want to get a room?"

That seemed to snap her out of her haze, because she doubled up her fists against his chest and pushed him away hard. She tugged down the hem of her rumpled, rain-soaked sweater with all the dignity of a queen, pushed a hand through her damp hair, and peered at him over the frames of her fogged-up spectacles. "I'm here looking for your daughter," she told him sharply.

He came *this* close to telling her she was adorable when she was angry, thought better of it, and instead told her, "So am I. And something tells me she's holed up here with my Walkman, the holiday issue of *Seventeen* magazine, a twelve-hour supply of Diet Coke and nachos, and an L.A. phone book, charging the whole thing to my American Express account."

Maddy's eyebrows arrowed down in a clear display of confusion. "What are you talking about? She was frantic when she called me."

"She sounded frantic when she called me, too."

Maddy shook her head. "I don't understand. She told me she'd had a fight with you. That she was afraid to go home. Why would she call you? Why would she call us both?"

Carver shoved his hands deep into the pockets of his jeans because he knew he was going to reach for her again if he didn't. "Look around, Maddy. What do you see?"

Warily, suspiciously, she did as he instructed. "I see the lobby of a bed-and-breakfast, why?"

"It's a nice place, isn't it?"

She eyed him more suspiciously. "Yes."

"A very *romantic* place, right?"

Maddy surveyed their surroundings again. "I suppose so. What does that have to do with anything?"

Instead of answering her, Carver turned to the desk clerk. "Do you have a reservation for Carver Venner?"

The harried-looking little man searched quickly through a box of index cards and seemed relieved when he located what he was looking for. "Here it is. A reservation for Mr. and Mrs. Carver Venner. Room seventeen. Your luggage has already been taken up. I'll just need for you to fill out this card and sign by the X. Do you want to leave the room on your American Express?"

Maddy's glance darted from the man she had been berating back to Carver. "Mr. and Mrs.?" she repeated. "Complete with luggage? Just what's this all about anyway? What are you trying to pull, Carver?"

Without responding to Maddy, he reached into his back pocket for his wallet, opened it, and sifted through a small selection of credit cards. "Yep, it's missing," he said as he completed the action a second time. "Man, that kid is some piece of work." He turned to the desk clerk. "The signature on that card is nontransferable, you know."

"She hasn't signed anything yet," the man told him. "She said you'd be here to do that."

Carver turned to Maddy again with a resigned shrug. "Can my kid call 'em, or can she call 'em, huh?"

Still looking confused, Maddy opened her mouth to say something, but the desk clerk prevented her by making another announcement.

"Oh, and your daughter left a message for you, too."

He extended a piece of paper toward Carver that Maddy snatched from his hand and opened. He looked over her shoulder and read along with her.

Hi, guys,
Thanks for coming to my rescue. The least I can do is return the favor. I checked out your room before I reserved it, and it's really nice. You're lucky. You got the last one. Lanette and I are on another floor. By now we've siphoned the gas from your cars. And AAA doesn't service this part of the county. I checked. It's a pretty crummy night for walking, so you might as well just stay here until morning. The rooms have fireplaces. And they leave these cute little chocolates on your pillow at night. It's the coolest thing. Anyway, have fun. They'll be bringing you some stuff to eat after you get settled in. See you in the morning.

Love, Rachel

"'Love, Rachel'?" Maddy repeated.

"She's starting to feel more comfortable with expressions of affection," Carver said. "I think it's very encouraging."

Maddy eyed him narrowly and turned to the desk clerk again. "What room is she in?"

He hedged, inspecting a worn spot on the desk. "She, uh...she asked me not to say."

"And she probably slipped you twenty bucks in the process to help you keep your word, didn't she?" Carver asked wryly.

This time the desk clerk studied his fingernails. "Actually, it was fifty."

Carver gaped at the man. "Fifty bucks? Where did she get fifty bucks?" He rubbed his chin thoughtfully. "Starting next week, I'm cutting that kid's allowance in half."

"Carver, don't you realize what Rachel's done?" Maddy demanded. "She's stranded us here."

He smiled at her. "Yeah, she's brought us back together but good, hasn't she?"

Maddy didn't like the warm, wonderful look Carver was giving her. She liked even less the warm, wonderful feelings that look sent spinning throughout her nervous system. "We are *not* back together," she told him.

"We are for the night. Unless you want to sleep down here on the lobby sofa."

Maddy dropped her gaze to the floor. "Being a gentleman, I thought you might offer to do that."

Carver chuckled and reached for the card the desk clerk had pushed toward him. Hastily, he filled it out, then scrawled his signature across the bottom. "You forget who you're talking to, Maddy. I'm no gentleman. Yeah, you can keep it on my card," he added for the desk clerk as he took the key the other man dangled from his fingers. "Where's room seventeen?"

"Up the stairs, to your right. About four doors down."

"Thanks. Maddy? You coming?"

Without awaiting her reply, Carver made his way toward the sweeping stairway at the lobby's center. Maddy watched him go, wondering how on earth she'd allowed herself to get roped into this. Her gaze skittered to the sofa near the stairs and lingered there for a moment. It was small and lumpy-looking and in no way private. She looked at Carver again, at the way the taut muscles of his thighs and calves were molded so lovingly by his wet blue jeans. When he reached the stairs, he took them two at a time, as if he couldn't wait to get comfortable in front of a nice, hot fire with a nice, mellow glass of wine.

A hot fire really did sound good, she thought. Not to mention a nice glass of wine. And a bath, she mused further, noting absently that she, too, had started to approach the stairs. A hot bath was exactly what she needed right now.

Tomorrow she could confront Rachel Stillman and demand to know what tonight's escapades were all about. Then Maddy, too, took the stairs two at a time as she ascended. She chose not to think yet about the confrontation she would have to face tonight.

Eleven

It was just the fire, that was all. The fire and the wine. The fire and the wine and the candlelight. The fire, the wine, the candlelight...and maybe the little chocolates on the pillows. Okay, the romantic furnishings in general. But that was all it was. That was the only reason Maddy was sitting on the divan staring at Carver on the other side of the room, wondering what it would be like to go over there, untie the loosely bound sash of his robe and run her hands all over his naked body. It had nothing to do with him.

She belted the sash of her own robe more tightly and studied the floral pattern of the sofa. *Luggage,* she repeated to herself with a sneer as she did so. Their luggage had consisted of one overnight bag Rachel had packed herself with all the necessary accoutrements for one romantic evening. A twelve-year-old's idea of what constituted the necessary accoutrements for one romantic evening, anyway. Maddy glanced down at her robe again. It was too short, too thin, too frilly and too pink. She couldn't remember the last time she'd worn pink. It must have been almost twenty years ago.

The only reason she had put the robe on was because her clothes were so wet and clammy from the rain. That and because the nightie beneath it, which Rachel had also so graciously provided, was even worse than the robe itself. Oh, well. At least the girl had gotten the size right. The pink mules with the marabou trim, however, were a bit too big. For that reason, along with the fact that Maddy found the shoes simply too ridiculous to even consider wearing them, she remained barefoot.

Carver, too, was shoeless, and his bare legs extended from beneath the hem of his paisley robe as he lounged on the floor in front of the fireplace. The two of them had spoken scarcely a word to each other since entering the room, and had looked at each other even less. What a bizarre scenario, Maddy thought. A beautiful, romantic inn, a softly crackling fire, a dark and stormy night, a gorgeous, sexy man...mellow red wine, candlelight... And all she could do was sit there in a state of confusion.

"You know, I always wondered what it would be like to stay in a place like this," Carver said softly from the other side of the room, as if it were just dawning on him, too, where they were.

Maddy twirled her glass by the stem and watched the ruby contents sheet on the side. "I would think a man like you would have stayed in places like this a dozen times at least."

He expelled a sound of resolution. "A man like me, huh? And just what kind of man am I, Maddy?"

She sipped her wine and thought to herself that there was no way to answer his question. Carver Venner defied both description and definition. It was as simple as that.

He must have taken her silence to mean that she was still angry, because when he continued, his voice was even softer and more cajoling than it had been before. "The kinds of places I stay in are usually pretty sparse on the furnishings. If I'm lucky, sometimes they have a shower. More often, they don't. A lot of times, they're under fire. One was even *on* fire," he added with a chuckle. He sobered when he turned to look at her. "And none of them has ever come complete with a beautiful woman."

This time Maddy was the one to chuckle. "Yeah, right. You must think I'm pretty gullible if you think I'll believe that."

She still refused to look directly at him, and only noticed from the corner of her eye when he rose from his seat and crossed the room toward her. When he stood beside the sofa, she continued to gaze elsewhere, at everything in the room except him. He was close enough that she imagined she could feel the heat of the fire radiating from him, and he smelled of wood smoke and bath soap and man. Her eyelids fluttered downward, and helplessly, she inhaled a great breath of him and held it as long as she dared.

"I've never thought you were gullible," he told her. "I've always thought you were..."

She opened her eyes again and glanced up at him, completely forgetting that she had meant to spend the evening ignoring him. "What?" she asked. "You've always thought I was what?"

In the soft light of the fire and candles, she could make out every line, every angle in his face. A lock of hair fell across his forehead like a dark shadow, and the hollows of his cheeks compounded what was already a menacing-looking gaze. His blue eyes glistened as they caught the flickering flame of the candle and seemed to fuel it. She had never seen a more beautiful man. And she wished more than anything that she could go back in time. Back twenty years, when the world had been such a perfect place. How differently things might have turned out.

She continued to watch him as he lifted one shoulder in a halfhearted shrug. "Extraordinary," he finally said quietly. "I always thought you were extraordinary."

Maddy let her gaze fall back to her glass. "You never thought that about me."

Carver dropped to his knees at her side. "What else would you call someone who continued to see the best in people when there were almost no examples of goodness to be found? What else would you call someone who kept on working to fulfill a dream and achieve a goal in spite of a million obstacles? Who got worn down to a shadow of a human being by the very society she was trying to fix, but who kept trying to improve it anyway?"

"Stupid, that's what I'd call her," Maddy said before sipping her wine again. She held the warm fluid in her mouth for a long time, savoring the sharp flavor because she had so little else to savor in life. When she finally swallowed, she added, "I'd call her stupid and naive."

He ignored her conclusion and said instead, "It's cold over here. Why don't we go sit closer to the fire?"

"You go. I'm fine."

"Liar." He stroked his finger up the length of her arm, beneath the sleeve of her robe. "You have goose bumps."

Maddy was about to tell him that her goose bumps had nothing to do with the cool air in the room, that she'd been plenty warm ever since Carver had stepped out of the bathroom in nothing but silk boxer shorts a half hour ago. Even when he'd thankfully tossed his robe on over his intriguing underwear, her body temperature had continued to rise. She didn't need to get closer to the fire to warm up. She was plenty close to Carver's fire now. If she got any warmer, she was going to spontaneously combust.

He continued to run his fingers along the length of her arm, up and down, back and forth, circling her wrist and cradling her hand in his. "Your hands are freezing," he said as he stood. "Come on over by the fire."

She allowed him to tug her up behind him and lead her across the room. Then, when she sat on the floor in front of the fireplace, she reached behind herself to pull down a cushion from a nearby chair and clutched it to her chest. She wanted to hold on to something—namely Carver, she had to confess—and a chair cushion seemed a likely enough substitute. Until she held it close and realized it was malleable and infirm, its fabric cool and rough to the touch. It was nothing at all like Carver. She set the cushion aside.

"I did always think you were extraordinary, you know."

When she looked at him, he was staring into the fire, talking to it instead of her, even though his words were clearly intended for her to hear.

"I always admired you," he continued in a quiet voice, still not looking at her. "Your optimism in the face of so much adversity was probably the only thing that kept me from getting completely mired down in my own bleak outlook on life. Without you, I probably would have just kissed off everyone and everything and hitched a ride to wherever I could make myself numb for the rest of my life. Instead, I went to college. You're responsible for that, Maddy. You made me think change was possible. You made me go about trying to affect a little myself."

Finally he turned toward her, studying her with a grave intensity when he spoke. "That was probably why I kissed you that time backstage. Because, even back then, I loved you for being the kind of person you were."

When Maddy felt something warm and wet on her face, she lifted a hand to her cheek. She was stunned to discover she was crying. She hadn't cried for... God, it had been years since she'd shed a tear. Except for once, she recalled now. That night when Carver came to her house to ask for her help in finding his daughter. She'd cried that night, she remembered. Something about Carver just made her feel things again, she supposed.

Quickly she brushed the dampness from her face, removed her glasses and rubbed her eyes hard.

"That's a nice thing to say," she told him quietly. "I don't believe you for a minute, but it's a nice thing to say."

"I don't care if you believe me or not. I loved you back then, Maddy. It's just taken me twenty years to realize it."

She sniffled and met his gaze levelly. "Well, if it's true, then I'm sorry. Because I'm not the person you loved anymore. And I'll never be that girl again. If you loved Maddy Saunders, Carver, then you're out of luck. She just doesn't exist anymore."

"I'm not convinced of that. If the Maddy I'm sitting here with now is so different from the Maddy I knew in high school, then how come you're still trying to make a difference in the world as a social worker after all this time?"

"Who says I'm making a difference? I don't make a difference. There's still poverty and crime and viciousness everywhere you look. It gets worse every year. Kids still get lost, they still get hurt and they still get killed. It will always be that way. Nothing I can do will change that."

"If you really believe that, then why don't you just quit your job and do something else? Something that will bring you happiness and fulfillment? Why don't you teach or write or plant flowers, for God's sake? Why don't you just chuck the Child Welfare Office and look for something at F.A.O. Schwarz instead?"

His question was one Maddy had asked herself hundreds of times. And she was no closer to having an answer now than she had been years ago when the thought had first entered her brain. She didn't know why she kept putting herself through the motions every day when those motions never seemed to make a difference. She didn't know why she kept getting out of bed and performing the requirements of a job that got her nowhere. She didn't know what kept her going. But it wasn't optimism; of that she was quite confident. And it certainly wasn't hope.

"I'll grant you that the world can be a truly ugly place," Carver continued when she said nothing to contradict him. "And it's populated in places by a lot of horrible people. And, unfortunately, it will probably always be that way."

He rose to his knees and moved to sit beside her, taking her hands in his. "But there are also some safe little pockets of goodness out there, Maddy, the occasional places where decency and honor sometimes win out."

"Maybe," she conceded. She watched idly as he threaded his fingers through hers, and she tried to ignore the warm tingle of satisfaction that wound up her arm as a result. Unfortunately, his gesture only made her want to draw closer to him. So she tried verbally to push him away. "But what good are those places when—"

"What good are they?" he interrupted, tightening his fingers with hers. "I'll tell you what good they are. They're havens for people like you and me." He dipped his head to hers and nuzzled her ear as he whispered, "People who are too stupid and naive to realize they can't possibly make a difference, yet manage to affect change because of that very ignorance."

He traced a line of delicate kisses from her ear to her jaw, from her jaw to her mouth. "People like us need a place to retreat to every now and then so we can regroup," he told her before pressing his lips to hers again. When he pulled away after a chaste brush of his mouth over hers, he added, "Thank God you and I found each other after all this time. Because who else have we had to turn to in the last twenty years?"

No one, Maddy realized. No one at all. And maybe that was the problem. Maybe that was why she had lost hope.

Without questioning what she was doing, she turned until she faced him, until she could look fully upon the man who had once caused her to feel so much frustration, anger, resentment, fascination, affection and more. Carver Venner had probably made her feel more things, more intensely, than any other human being ever had. Without him in her life, she had gradually ceased to feel at all. Bit by bit, she had been whittled down to a shell of a human being. A human being who cared little for anything. Who cared even less about herself.

A burst of recognition lit the dark corners of her mind, and she laughed a little uncertainly. "That's it, isn't it?" she said quietly. "That's been it all along."

He seemed puzzled, but encouraged. "What's it?"

"You. You and Rachel. Ever since her file landed on my desk, ever since I saw your name on her birth certificate, I've had this hope that things would work out between the two of you. That you'd succeed. I cared about what happened to you. I hoped for the best."

"Don't you always feel that way about a case?"

She shook her head and said softly, "No. I don't. I know that sounds terrible, but I never have any hope that a case is going to turn out for the best, because they so seldom do. I learned a long time ago to stop caring about the outcome, because I just kept feeling more and more crushed every time a case went sour."

She held up his hand to stop his objection and assured him quickly, "Oh, sure, sometimes they work out fine. But when that happens, I don't feel vindicated—I feel surprised. With you and Rachel, for the first time in a long, long time, I hoped for the best. And the best is how it turned out."

She laughed again, feeling a little bubble of delight ripple through her. "You're right. I guess I do still have hope. I do still have a streak of optimism in me. I guess deep down, I haven't changed that much in twenty years. I've just managed to shut myself off for a while."

She felt her eyes filling again, but this time the tears were anything but sad. "And it's weird," she continued, "but I'm just beginning to realize something else. Back in high school, the two of us were a lot alike. In your own way, you thought you could make the world a better place, too. You just went about it a little more radically than I did."

She cupped her palm over his nape and pulled his forehead to hers. "And, in a way, the two of us are a lot alike now. We've both seen more of the world than we'd care to see. We both condemn it. And we're both still stupid enough to think we can make a difference."

"We already have made a difference," Carver pointed out. "In one life, anyway—Rachel's. She came to us an insecure, unstructured, undisciplined little brat. Now look at her—she's playing matchmaker to a couple of old fools. We only have ourselves to blame for getting stranded tonight. We're the ones who made Rachel realize that we do in fact care about her. As a result, she's learning to care about us."

"Maybe she sees something we don't," Maddy said.

"Speak for yourself. I see plenty."

Maddy smiled. "Rachel can be our reminder that you and I—when we work together—can make a difference somewhere. Her life ahead holds promise now, instead of a big question mark, which is all she had before. Because of you and me, Rachel's going to have a happy ending."

Carver smiled back. "Why should Rachel be the only one?"

And with that he leaned in again, touching his mouth to Maddy's only long enough to stir her into agitation.

"I love you, Maddy," he said when he pulled away. "And have for more than twenty years. Tell me you love me, too."

"I love you, too."

Carver was surprised that she would reassure him so readily. Not that he hadn't been confident all along of Maddy's feelings for him. He'd just been expecting her to fight them a little bit longer. "You do?" he said.

She nodded. "I suppose, in a way, I've loved you for twenty years, too. Certainly no other man has made me feel the things you do."

He wiggled his eyebrows suggestively. "Oh, yeah? Like what? Feel free to give me specific examples."

She smiled. "Oh, like . . . infuriated . . . ticked off . . . exasperated . . ."

He kissed her briefly before adding, "Crazy with desire . . . yearning for more . . ."

"Fed up . . . confounded . . . thoroughly confused—"

"Out of your head in love," he concluded.

She nodded. "Out of my head in love."

"So, what are we going to do about that?"

"Try to affect some change?" she asked.

He shook his head. "A change of clothes maybe... Although I kind of like you in all that pink lacy stuff. Makes you look like a big puff of cotton candy."

"Oh, Carver, please."

"Still, I am going to have to find out where my daughter's been getting some of her ideas lately. I've been wondering about all those *Sassy* magazines I've seen lying around the apartment. Whose idea was it anyway to name some magazine for girls *Sassy*? I don't think it's good for prepubescent girls to be sassy, do you? It's bad enough when women are sassy."

"Carver?"

"Yes?"

"Shut up and quit being so sassy."

He smiled. "Yes, ma'am. What did you have in mind?"

"I'd like to get out of this cotton candy suit. I feel like Frederick's of Hollywood Barbie in this thing."

"Then by all means, allow me to assist you."

He started by tucking his fingers beneath the sash of her robe, deftly unraveling the loose knot before curving his palms over her shoulders and skimming the soft fabric down her arms. Maddy felt a chill kiss of air ripple across her bare skin, only to be warmed by Carver's lips following in its wake. He kissed her shoulder, her neck, her ear, then dipped his head lower, to the soft hollow at the base of her throat. She curled her fingers over his shoulders, pushing away his robe, too, so that she could explore him as intimately.

He made her feel warm and wanton and wonderful. His skin beneath her fingertips came alive everywhere she touched him. Muscle and sinew seemed to dance in the firelight, bunching and relaxing like satin-clad, molten steel. Maddy tangled her fingers in his hair and pulled him nearer, opening her mouth over his throat to taste the salty sultriness of him, raking her flat palm down his back to urge him closer still.

Behind them, the fire leapt and snapped like a living thing, its heat enveloping the lovers in a blanket of golden light. Carver hooked his fingers beneath the straps of Maddy's gown and pulled them from her shoulders, and the confection of fabric pooled around her waist. He cupped his palms over both her breasts, flexing his fingers until his thumbs drew erratic circles over the dusky peaks. But his gaze never left hers, as if her eyes might reveal the secrets of the universe.

Maddy reached out to him, curling her fingers behind his nape, and pulled him down to her breasts. Immediately, Carver lifted one to his mouth, tasting her over and over, until she feared he would consume her whole. She tipped her head back in surrender, watching the play of light and shadow on the ceiling, falling deeper and deeper into the erotic spell that he cast. No one had ever made her feel the way Carver did, she thought vaguely. And no one ever would again.

She lost herself to him after that, surrendering that part of herself responsible for coherence, yielding utterly to her desires. She wanted to forget who she was, where she was, everything about her life. She wanted to make love with Carver until the sun dared to make an appearance again. She wanted the night to go on forever. She wanted...so much. So many things. She wanted to hold him forever.

He continued to trail feathery kisses over her breasts as he gently pushed her backward, cradling her head in one hand, her sleek derriere in the other. Side by side, they explored each other more adventurously, their legs and arms a tangle, their mouths fused in a passion that built gradually into frenzy. Maddy nudged her hand below the waistband of his boxers, cupping her hand possessively over his taut buttocks before pushing the garment away completely. His calves and thighs were hard and hot as she raked her fingers back up along their length, just as she knew the rest of him would be.

She bent to kiss his ribs one by one, tracing with her tongue the rigid hills and valleys of muscle that decorated his abdomen. As she explored him, Carver took advantage of her position to push the rest of her clothing from her body. Then they lay naked, gazing at each other in the firelight, smiling, caressing, and feeling very, very warm.

Wordlessly, Carver reached for Maddy, lowering her to the rug beneath him, draping his body over hers. The weight and heat of him sinking into her torso and between her legs made her feel as though she were being welcomed home. But as quickly as the satisfied sensation settled inside her, it began to shatter. Because Carver traced an idle finger along her hip, skimming it over the graceful curves of her fanny before dipping between her thighs.

"Oh," she murmured softly. "Oh, Carver."

Without preamble, he stroked her soft folds once and entered her, foraging to make way for a more thorough exploration. Maddy arched her back toward him, inviting him to investigate more completely, and Carver accommodated her request. Just as she felt herself hovering at the apex of completion, he shifted himself slightly, and a more demanding part of him joined with her. He entered her slowly, deeply, and with much deliberation. And then, with a fervent, unfocused, almost uncontrolled fury, he drove her to the brink of insanity.

The flame and heat of the fire in the fireplace whispered into nothingness compared to the conflagration raging inside Maddy. Carver, too, seemed fueled by their union, and his flesh felt searing beneath her fingertips. Together, they ignited, together they burned. Together, they became incandescent. Then, in an explosive burst of white-hot combustion, they became one. And somehow, vaguely, deep inside Maddy's soul, she knew she would never be separate from Carver again.

He cried out as they climaxed together, words of passion, words of love. Maddy wanted to say the words back to him, wanted to tell him she loved him, too. But something inside her silenced her. She was too weak, she decided, too spent and exhausted to be able to do anything but feel. She loved Carver, of that there was no doubt. Yet for some reason, she couldn't tell him so.

Instead, she splayed her hands open over his slick, warm back, softly tracing his spine and rib cage. She kissed his neck, his ear, his cheek. She asked him if he was all right and felt him nod his response. She nodded, too. But somehow, she knew she wasn't all right. There was something else, she recalled in a fuzzy, ill-defined memory. Something the two of them hadn't settled. She just couldn't quite remember what it was. And at the moment, she had to confess, she really didn't care.

She turned her face to his and kissed him hard, then felt him swell to life inside her again. She smiled at him. He smiled back. And with a few deceptively calm touches, they roused the inferno again.

Tomorrow, Maddy thought as she rolled Carver to his back and straddled him. She would worry about it tomorrow. Cognitive thought had no place in what she wanted to do to him now. She reached for the part of him that had given her so much pleasure only moments ago. Tomorrow would be soon enough to think.

Twelve

It wasn't a door slamming that awoke Carver this time, but rather the soft, rapid brush of knuckles on the door. When he first opened his eyes, he wasn't sure whether he'd heard anything at all. Then he turned his head toward the sound and saw a slip of paper scooting beneath the door. The gray light in the room told him it was still quite early, and the rain spattering quietly against the windows told him it was still quite cloudy. The previous evening's fire smoldered in the fireplace, but it scarcely provided enough warmth for the room. He snuggled closer to Maddy, who continued to sleep peacefully beside him.

She smelled wonderful, he thought as he nuzzled the soft skin of her neck. Smoky and womanly and sweet. She moaned quietly when he lingered his kisses at her jaw, then turned her body more fully into his. He pressed his mouth to hers before reluctantly pushing himself away.

"Where are you going?" she murmured as he padded his

way naked across the room. She squinted at the clock. "What time is it?"

He bent to retrieve the scrap of paper beneath the door, but in the dim light couldn't quite make out what it said. So he returned to bed, kissed Maddy again, and switched on a lamp beside them.

"It's just past six," he told her as he scanned the note from his daughter. "According to this missive from Rachel, it's time for us to be getting up. She's planning on joining us for breakfast in fifteen minutes."

A quick knock at the door startled them both. "Or less," he amended.

"Hey, you guys," Rachel called from the other side, "it's me. Wake up. Let's eat."

"Uh, Rachel," Carver called back, noting not quite from the corner of his eye how far the sheet had fallen from Maddy's shoulders when she'd pushed herself up from the bed. "Can't this wait awhile? It's awfully early." He touched his finger to Maddy's breast to draw an idle circle, and she sighed. "How about if we meet you and Lanette in the dining room at, oh, say... ten?"

"Can't," Rachel told them. "Lanette's mom already picked her up, and I have basketball practice at nine. Remember how happy you were when I made the team? You don't want me to tick off Coach Carmichael, do you?"

"Oh, Carver," Maddy moaned softly beside him, her voice scarcely audible. "You have to stop that immediately or Rachel's going to hear something she really shouldn't."

By now he had completely covered her breast with his hand and was urging it toward his mouth. Rachel's announcement and Maddy's softly uttered plea stopped him cold, however. Because slowly, very slowly, he realized that if he kept this up, he would be making love to Maddy while his twelve-year-old daughter listened in.

"Carver? Maddy?" Rachel called from the other side of the door. She jiggled the doorknob meaningfully. "Come on, open up. I don't have that much time."

He scrambled from beneath the covers and prowled frantically around the room for his clothes. Maddy seemed to sense his urgency, because she, too, sprang from bed and raced to the bathroom to retrieve her clothes of the previous evening. Carver's jeans and sweater were still damp and cold, but he struggled into them anyway. All the while, Rachel's knocking and pleas for them to open the door sounded in his ears. But there was no way he was going anywhere near that door until they had all their clothes in place. One morning-after run-in with his daughter had already been one too many.

"Will you guys hurry up?" Rachel demanded. "Come on. I mean, hey, it's not like I don't know what you've been doing in there all night, anyway."

Carver's ears pricked up at that, but he said nothing.

"I know what happens when a man and woman fall in love," Rachel added. "I know all about what they do after that."

Carver's struggles ceased immediately. Rachel knew what happened when a man and woman fell in love? he repeated to himself. She knew all about the mechanics of sex? But she was only twelve years old. How could she know all about that?

He glanced quickly at Maddy to make sure she was all buttoned up, and found her smoothing the worst of the mountains and valleys out of the sheets. Satisfied that the two of them had reasonably hidden any vestige of their previous night's adventures, Carver snatched open the door. Rachel stood on the other side, wearing a plaid pleated skirt and black T-shirt, black tights, and huge, clunky black boots. She was also wearing a big grin. Okay, so maybe she still didn't dress the way he remembered twelve-year-olds from his time dressing, he thought, but she didn't look like a bum anymore, either. Not like the bums he knew, anyway.

"Just what the he..." He sighed and tried again. "Just what on earth do you know about...about...about what happens to a man and a woman when they fall in love?"

Rachel rolled her eyes at him in exactly the same way she had the first day he had met her. This time, however, her expression seemed to indicate that she didn't think him a moron so much as she did hopelessly naive.

"They get married," she said as she pushed past him into the room. "What else? Hi, Maddy."

"Hello, Rachel," Maddy replied automatically. But her gaze was fastened on Carver.

"So, do you have the wedding plans all made out yet or not?" Rachel asked.

Carver continued to look at Maddy, who continued to gaze right back at him.

"Uh, actually, Rachel..." he began. But he never made it any further.

"I want to be a junior bridesmaid," Rachel interrupted him. "*Sassy* says you can do that when you're twelve. You can be a junior bridesmaid. I know a dress I like. It's hot pink taffeta. And it's only 350 bucks. Pretty cool, huh?"

Carver didn't know what to contradict first. That he and Maddy hadn't made a single wedding plan or that there was no way on God's green earth that he was buying his daughter a dress that was that expensive.

"Uh, actually, Rachel," he tried again, "Maddy and I haven't, um..." He looked at Maddy again. "Have we?" he asked her a little uncertainly.

Her eyebrows shot up in surprise. "Have we what?" she asked.

"Well, have you or haven't you?" Rachel demanded.

Carver smiled before turning his attention to his daughter again. "We haven't discussed the wedding plans yet."

Rachel spat out a sound of incredulous disgust. "What? No wedding plans yet? Then what were you doing all night? Why do you think I got you guys here in the first place?" She went to the antique desk in the corner and pulled a pen and sheaf of stationery from the drawer. "We have to work fast. I'm starving, and this place is supposed to have killer Belgian waffles. Okay, Maddy, what color dress are you going to wear? White?"

"I...I...I..." Maddy's voice died off in a tremble. Her legs crumpled beneath her and she dropped to sit on the bed.

Rachel looked at her curiously. "What's the matter? You don't like white?"

"I...it's just that..." She sighed, searched Carver's face again in a silent bid for help, and shook her head.

"Maddy's been married before," Carver told his daughter, still grinning. "So she probably wants to avoid white."

Rachel raised a hand palm up. "Say no more. Not to worry. Ivory will look better with your complexion anyway."

"Carver, we have to talk," Maddy said softly.

He nodded before turning to Rachel. "Could you just give us about ten minutes, kiddo?"

"But—"

He took Rachel's hand and tugged her up from her seat at the desk, then gently cajoled her toward the door. "Why don't you go ahead and order some killer waffles for all of us, and Maddy and I will be right down?"

"But—"

"We just have a couple more things to iron out with the wedding plans, that's all."

Rachel made a face at both of them. "It takes you guys forever, doesn't it?"

Carver nodded. "Yeah. We're not quite as quick as we were when we were kids."

Rachel exited, pulling the door closed behind her, mumbling something about how that was the case with most grown-ups these days.

When Carver turned around, it was to find Maddy still seated on the bed looking haunted and fearful and lonely.

"What?" he asked as he neared her. He sat on the bed beside her, taking her cold hands in his. "What's wrong?"

"Carver, I can't marry you," she told him.

"What do you mean you can't marry me? Why not?"

She laughed softly, sounding very sad. "Well, for one thing, you haven't asked me."

He smacked his forehead at the oversight. "Sorry. Okay, Maddy, will you marry me?"

She shook her head. "No."

He told himself the galloping roar in his brain was the result of something harmless—like a busted artery or something—and nothing more. A couple of deep breaths and he'd be just fine. But after a couple of deep breaths, Maddy was still looking stricken and hopeless, and Carver didn't feel better at all.

"What's wrong?" he repeated. "Why won't you marry me?"

She took his hand in hers and squeezed it hard before lifting it to her lips. She kissed his palm softly, wove her fingers with his, then lowered their hands and pressed them over her flat belly.

"Because I'm empty," she told him. "I can't give you that family you want."

He shook his head at her as if she were the most dense creature he'd ever had the misfortune to meet. "Empty?" he repeated incredulously. "Maddy, you have more inside you than any human being I've ever met. More goodness, more kindness, more concern, more consideration, more hope, more love. If you were any fuller," he added with a chuckle, "there wouldn't be any room for anyone else in there. And I'm hoping you'll make room for someone else. Two someone elses. Me and Rachel.

"You *are* the family I want," he told her. "Don't you see? You and Rachel. The three of us make a good team. A good family. It's all I'll ever need. I'm hoping it's all you'll ever need, too."

She shook her head doubtfully. "You say it's enough now, but—"

"I say that now because it's true. What you and I have together feels good. It feels right. I can't imagine anything that would make it better, including children."

She didn't look convinced, but she still gripped his hand tightly in hers, as if she were reluctant to let him go.

He lifted his free hand to her forehead, brushing her hair away from her face. "Look, I know your first husband told you the same thing, but having more children isn't that important to me. Not nearly as important as you are. I don't know what to say to convince you of that. All I can say is...look what we have. Think about how we make each other feel. Remember how neither of us has felt quite complete in the years that we've been apart."

He tipped his head to hers. "I love you, Maddy. That's all there is to it. And I want to spend the rest of my life with you, if you'll have me. If you'll have me and Rachel. I know we're not the biggest prize in the world, but we love you. Just the way you are."

Maddy tangled her fingers in his hair and laughed. "As crazy as it sounds, I believe you. Don't ask me why, but I think you mean it when you say children aren't that big a deal for you." She kissed him softly and pulled briefly away. "And suddenly, for some reason, they're not that big a deal for me, either. Having you back...finding you and Rachel... It makes me feel full somehow. Complete. Satisfied." She kissed him again. "I've missed you all these years."

"I've missed you, too."

"It's good to see you again."

"It's good to see you, too."

They sat side by side, studying each other for some time before Carver broke the silence.

"So," he began slowly, softly, "you want to get married or what?"

Maddy grinned at him. "I suppose it would break Rachel's heart if she didn't get to plan our wedding."

"It would break mine, too."

"Then I guess that settles it."

"Good." He stood and tugged her up from the bed and into his arms. "What say we seal the deal over waffles? And maybe bacon and eggs, too. With all due respect to Rachel's kinder, gentler vegetarian life-style, I'd love to sink my teeth into something more substantial."

"Sounds good," Maddy agreed. "I'm starving."

"Really? Are you honestly going to eat something? Or are you just going to push your food around on the plate like you usually do?"

"Oh, believe me, I'm planning to put away three or four waffles, for starters. I've never been hungrier in my life." She tightened her fingers with his. "And that's only one appetite I have in mind to satisfy this morning." She leaned over to nibble his ear before whispering into it, "How long does Rachel's basketball practice usually last?"

Together, they crossed the room and opened the door, only to find Rachel on the other side, leaning against the doorjamb, shamelessly eavesdropping. "There's just one more thing I want to know," she told Maddy when she was discovered. "Are you going to change your name when you get married?"

Rachel's forwardness didn't surprise Maddy nearly as much as the question itself did. "I...I don't know. I haven't thought about it. I'm certainly not M. H. Garrett, jaded caseworker, anymore, thanks to you two." She gave Carver's hand another squeeze and pulled him closer. "But I'll never be Maddy Saunders again, either."

"Then be Maddy Venner," Rachel told her with a shrug.

She smiled. "That has a nice ring to it. Okay. I'll change my name to Venner."

Rachel nodded her approval. "Good. So will I."

Carver smiled, too, feeling a warm flush of love and pride wash over him. He brushed his fingertips briefly across his daughter's cheek. "Whatever you want, kiddo. Whatever you want."

"Then I can get my nose pierced, too?" she asked as he locked the door behind them.

"Except for that."

"But, Carver..."

"Don't you 'But, Carver' me, kid. I'm not going to fall for it."

Rachel tried a new approach. "But, Daddy..."

He smiled. "You're getting closer. But it's still no."

"It's not like I'm getting a tattoo, you know," Rachel pointed out. "Although Lanette's mom has a great one on her ankle, a long-stemmed rose."

"No, Rachel."

"But, Daddy..."

"I said, no."

Rachel turned to Maddy with a smile. "Mom?" she asked. "What do you think?"

Maddy eyed them both warily. "I think it's going to take a while to get used to this family."

Carver and Rachel looked first at each other, then at Maddy, both breaking out in wide smiles.

"It's a good family," Rachel assured her. "You'll like it. You just have to remember to follow the rules. I hope you don't smoke..."

Carver wrapped one arm around Maddy, the other around Rachel, kissing each one on the cheek. He wondered how on earth he'd ever gotten so lucky, decided not to worry about it, and led them toward the stairs. Together, the three of them went down to breakfast. They were going to need a big meal to start the rest of their lives off right.

* * * * *

SILHOUETTE® Desire®

COMING NEXT MONTH

It's Silhouette Desire's 1000th birthday! Join us for a spectacular three-month celebration, starring your favorite authors and the hottest heroes of the decade!

#997 BABY DREAMS—Raye Morgan

The Baby Shower

Sheriff Rafe Lonewolf couldn't believe his feisty new prisoner was the innocent woman she claimed to be. But a passionate night with Cami Bishop was suddenly making *him* feel criminal!

#998 THE UNWILLING BRIDE—Jennifer Greene

The Stanford Sisters

Paige Stanford's new neighbor was sexy, smart...and single! Little did she know Stefan Michaelovich wanted to make *her* his blushing bride!

#999 APACHE DREAM BRIDE—Joan Elliott Pickart

When Kathy Maxwell purchased a dream catcher, she had no idea she'd soon catch herself an Apache groom! But could her dream really come true...or would she have to give up the only man she ever loved?

#1000 MAN OF ICE—Diana Palmer

Silhouette Desire #1000!

After one tempestuous night with irresistible Barrie Bell, May's MAN OF THE MONTH, Dawson Rutherford, swore off love forever. Now the only way he could get the land he wanted was to make Barrie his temporary bride.

#1001 INSTANT HUSBAND—Judith McWilliams

The Wedding Night

Nick St. Hilarion needed a mother for his daughter, not a woman for himself to love! But when Ann Lennon arrived special delivery, he realized he might not be able to resist falling for his mail-order wife!

#1002 BABY BONUS—Amanda Kramer

Debut Author

Leigh Townsend was secretly crazy about sexy Nick Romano, but she wasn't going to push him to propose! So she didn't tell him he was going to be a daddy—or else he would insist on becoming a husband, too.

SILHOUETTE®

Desire®

CELEBRATION 1000

A treasured piece of romance could be yours!

During April, May and June as part of
Desire's Celebration 1000 you can enter to win an
original piece of art used on an actual Desire cover!

Or you could win one of 300 autographed Man of the
Month books!

See Official Sweepstakes Rules for more details.

To enter, complete an Official Entry Form or a 3"x5" card by hand printing
"Silhouette Desire Celebration 1000 Sweepstakes", your name and address, and
mail to: **In the U.S.:** Silhouette Desire Celebration 1000 Sweepstakes, P.O. Box
9069, Buffalo, N.Y. 14269-9069, or **In Canada:** Silhouette Desire Celebration 1000
Sweepstakes, P.O. Box 637, Fort Erie, Ontario L2A 5X3. Limit one entry per
envelope. Entries must be sent via first-class mail and be received no later than
6/30/96. No liability is assumed for lost, late or misdirected mail.

**Official Entry Form—Silhouette Desire Celebration 1000
Sweepstakes**

Name: _____

Address: _____

City: _____

State/Province: _____

Zip or Postal Code: _____

Favorite Desire Author: _____

Favorite Desire Book: _____

SWEEPS

SILHOUETTE DESIRE® "CELEBRATION 1000" SWEEPSTAKES
OFFICIAL RULES—NO PURCHASE NECESSARY

To enter, complete an Official Entry Form or a 3"x5" card by hand printing "Silhouette Desire Celebration 1000 Sweepstakes," your name and address, and mail it to: In the U.S.: Silhouette Desire Celebration 1000 Sweepstakes, P.O. Box 9069, Buffalo, NY 14269-9069, or in Canada: Silhouette Desire Celebration 1000 Sweepstakes, P.O. Box 637, Fort Erie, Ontario L2A 5X3. Limit one entry per envelope. Entries must be sent via first-class mail and be received no later than 6/30/96. No liability is assumed for lost, late or misdirected mail.

Prizes: Grand Prize—an original painting (approximate value $1500 U.S.);300 Runner-up Prizes—an autographed Silhouette Desire® Book (approximate value $3.50 U.S./$3.99 CAN. each). Winners will be selected in a random drawing (to be conducted no later than 9/30/96) from among all eligible entries received by D.L. Blair, Inc., an independent judging organization whose decision is final.

Sweepstakes offer is open only to residents of the U.S. (except Puerto Rico) and Canada who are 18 years of age or older, except employees and immediate family members of Harlequin Enterprises Ltd., their affiliates, subsidiaries, and all agencies, entities and persons connected with the use, marketing or conduct of this sweepstakes. All federal, state, provincial, municipal and local laws apply. Offer void where prohibited by law. Taxes and/or duties are the sole responsibility of the winners. Any litigation within the province of Quebec respecting the conduct and awarding of prizes may be submitted to the Regie des alcools des courses et des jeux. All prizes will be awarded; winners will be notified by mail. No substitution for prizes is permitted. Odds of winning are dependent upon the number of eligible entries received.

Grand Prize winner must sign and return an Affidavit of Eligibility within 30 days of notification. In the event of noncompliance within this time period, prize may be awarded to an alternate winner. Any prize or prize notification returned as undeliverable may result in the awarding of that prize to an alternate winner. By acceptance of their prize, winners consent to the use of their names, photographs or likenesses for purposes of advertising, trade and promotion on behalf of Harlequin Enterprises Ltd., without further compensation unless prohibited by law. In order to win a prize, residents of Canada will be required to correctly answer a time-limited arithmetical skill-testing question administered by mail.

For a list of winners (available after October 31, 1996) send a separate self-addressed stamped envelope to: Silhouette Desire Celebration 1000 Sweepstakes Winners, P.O. Box 4200, Blair, NE 68009-4200.

SWEEPR

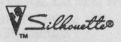

BEGINNING IN APRIL
FROM

SILHOUETTE® Desire®

DEBUT AUTHOR

In April, May and June we'll be celebrating the publication of Silhouette Desire's 1000th book! And each month will feature a brand-new writer you're sure to be excited about.

In April—
TWO WEDDINGS AND A BRIDE by Anne Eames

In May—
BABY BONUS by Amanda Kramer

In June—
THE LONER AND THE LADY by Eileen Wilks

Don't miss these stars of tomorrow—
premiering today!

They're the hardest working, sexiest women in the Lone Star State...they're

Annette Broadrick

The O'Brien sisters: Megan, Mollie and Maribeth. Meet them and the men who want to capture their hearts in these titles from Annette Broadrick:

MEGAN'S MARRIAGE
(February, Silhouette Desire #979)

The *MAN OF THE MONTH* is getting married to *very* reluctant bride Megan O'Brien!

INSTANT MOMMY
(March, Silhouette Romance #1139)

A *BUNDLE OF JOY* brings Mollie O'Brien together with the man she's always loved.

THE GROOM, I PRESUME?
(April, Silhouette Desire #992)

Maribeth O'Brien's been left at the altar—but this bride won't have to wait long for wedding bells to ring!

Don't miss the DAUGHTERS OF TEXAS—three brides waiting to lasso the hearts of their very own cowboys! Only from

SILHOUETTE® Desire   and   Silhouette ROMANCE™

DOT